Beethoven

Emily thrust the puppy into Mr Newton's face. 'Daddy, can we call him Fred?'

The puppy licked Mr Newton's face enthusiastically and barked a happy bark. He was home at last!

'Let's take him outside!' yelled Emily. The three Newton children ran out of the kitchen door, giggling happily.

Mrs Newton stayed behind with her husband. George looked shellshocked and horrified. There was *no way* a dog could fit into the Newton family scheme of things.

'There has been a terrible mistake,' he managed to stammer. 'I didn't have anything to do with getting that dog. It must be a stray. I'll have to take it down to the pound.'

Danielle Gibson

Beethoven

A novel by Robert Tine

Based on the screenplay by
Edmond Dantes and Amy Holden Jones

PUFFIN BOOKS

PUFFIN BOOKS

Published by the Penguin Group
Penguin Books Ltd, 27 Wrights Lane, London W8 5TZ, England
Penguin Books USA Inc., 375 Hudson Street, New York, New York 10014, USA
Penguin Books Australia Ltd, Ringwood, Victoria, Australia
Penguin Books Canada Ltd, 10 Alcorn Avenue, Toronto, Ontario, Canada M4V 3B2
Penguin Books (NZ) Ltd, 182–190 Wairau Road, Auckland 10, New Zealand

Penguin Books Ltd, Registered Offices: Harmondsworth, Middlesex, England

Puffin Film and TV Tie-in edition first published 1992
3 5 7 9 10 8 6 4 2

Typeset by DatIX International Limited, Bungay, Suffolk
Printed in England by Clays Ltd, St Ives plc

CHAPTER ONE

Of all the stores on the main street of Vista Valley, none got as many window-shoppers as the Land-O-Pets pet shop. Behind the glass were pens containing little puppies, who yipped and yapped and pawed at the windows, their big eyes begging the passers-by to come in and cuddle the small balls of fur, buy them and take them home. There were soft little cockers falling over their droopy ears, and next to them were lively Great Dane pups, and next to them were sweet – but dignified – springer spaniels. But the cutest dog, by far, was a brown and white St Bernard. Hardly anyone could pass that window without stopping to look at him.

'Aren't they sweet!' exclaimed a teenage girl.

'Yeah, they're cute at this age, but wait till they grow up!' said her boyfriend.

'That one is a boy,' said the girl, pointing at the St Bernard.

'How can you tell?'

'By the size of his paws!'

The couple peered at the little dog. He certainly hadn't grown into his big paws. He jumped against the glass and slid down, stumbling against his water-dish and tumbling into the straw that lined his cage.

The boy and girl laughed. 'Bye, honey . . .' They continued down the street.

The St Bernard barked and scratched at the glass, his pink tongue hanging from his mouth and his tail slapping frantically. He barked as loud as he could, as if to say, 'Don't go! Take me home with you!'

The teenage couple were soon replaced by other onlookers, including two boys who always liked to look in the pet-shop window.

'Hey,' said one of them, catching sight of the adorable little pup. 'He's cool.'

The St Bernard jumped against the glass and yapped, as if to say, 'That's right! I'm cool!'

'I think he likes us,' said the boy's companion. 'He really likes us!'

The pup was up on his stumpy hind legs, barking his head off as if trying to prove them right. 'Take me home! Take me home!'

But the puppy was to be disappointed once again. The boys knew that they couldn't take a puppy home without permission from their mum and dad. The boys chuckled at the St Bernard's antics, but they had to move on. The little dog was let down, but he took it in his stride.

A baby girl toddled up to the window and looked in. It was love at first sight. She stared at the puppy and giggled. The puppy licked the glass as if trying to give the girl a big, wet kiss.

'Mommeeee!' squealed the toddler.

'Not today, honey,' said her mother, leading her gently away.

Dejection clouded the eyes of the little dog. He barked sadly and the corners of his mouth turned down. He whimpered in melancholy. Was there no one in Vista Valley who loved him enough to take him home?

Of course, the puppy wouldn't go with just anybody. One afternoon, a mean-looking woman with a tattoo and long fingernails came into the pet shop.

'I wanna see that St Bernard in the window,' she told one of the girls who worked in the shop.

The salesgirl loved the St Bernard puppy as much as everyone else, and she didn't think this person would be the proper owner, but the customer is always right . . .

The girl scooped the dog out of his cage and put him in the arms of the mean-looking woman.

'How big do these critters get to be?'

'At least a hundred and fifty pounds,' said the salesgirl. 'Sometimes even more.' She hoped that the size would scare her off. People didn't like to pay the money to feed a dog that big.

But her plan backfired. The woman smiled cruelly. 'That's good. I got a junkyard. I need to get a big, mean junkyard dog.'

The little pup wriggled, horrified, in the rough hands of the tattooed woman.

'Yeah,' she said, 'he looks good and mean to me.'

The puppy certainly didn't want to go with this person. He did his best to look sweeter and cuddlier than ever. He squirmed and licked and acted as friendly as possible. 'I'm not mean,' he was trying frantically to say. 'I *love* everybody. I could *never* be mean.'

'I don't know,' said the salesgirl, 'he's pretty sweet.'

The puppy whimpered as the woman held him by the scruff of the neck. They were eyeball to eyeball, the puppy wriggling, trying to get free. The woman grinned broadly. 'You can make any dog mean, ya know. Just gotta know how to treat 'em. Treat 'em rough.'

That was all the puppy needed to hear. This called for desperate measures. All of a sudden, there came a tinkling sound and the woman looked down to see that the dog was weeing on her.

'Little beast!' growled the woman. She slung the dog into the arms of the salesgirl. 'I ain't takin' him home. Put him away. Got any pit-bulls?'

The salesgirl put the dog back in his cage and he dived into the straw, heaving a sigh of relief as he did so. That was *close*, he thought.

Well, by the end of the day, he was still in his cage. It looked like he wasn't going to get a family that day. Night was falling and a storm was beginning to blow up. The puppy rested his head on his paws and sighed. It had been a long day.

Just before closing-time, a family came into the shop, a mother and father and a little boy. The small dog jumped to his feet and barked. Here they were! These were the people who were going to take him home. They looked so nice! He was going to be happy with them . . .

But they never looked at him. They walked right past his cage and stopped at the next one, which was occupied by a sweet black poodle.

'This is the one I want, Mom!' shouted the boy. He scooped up the warm little bundle and petted it.

The St Bernard looked sad and wistful. It wasn't his turn, not yet. He put his head down on his paws and yawned. Maybe tomorrow will be my lucky day, he thought, as he fell into a deep sleep.

CHAPTER TWO

There were dogs in cages at a place on the other side of town, but they weren't happy or hopeful the way the dogs in the pet shop were. These dogs were penned up in dirty, rusting cages stacked in a cold, dreary, damp warehouse. A sign outside the building said that it was home to Dandy Pup Pet Supply, but that was just a name that had been made up to disguise what really went on inside the grim old building.

The Dandy Pup Pet Supply warehouse was in a run-down part of town, an area that was also home to some old factories, scrapyards and the Vista Valley central market. No one in the neighbourhood knew or cared what really went on at Dandy Pup, and the owner and the two men who worked for him didn't tell anybody.

The real business of Dandy Pup Pet Supply was testing things on animals – illegal things, like drugs and guns. To prevent cruelty to animals, the government strictly controls what testing-companies can and cannot do. But Dandy Pup didn't play by the rules. Everything they did was unlawful.

The business was run by a man called Dr Varnick and he spent most of the time bossing around his two helpers, Vernon and Harvey. Of the two men,

Vernon was the smarter, but neither of them would have scored very highly in intelligence tests. Dr Varnick was in charge of the testing, and Vernon and Harvey handled the dogs and found ways of getting more of them for the doctor's evil experiments.

Vernon and Harvey took stray dogs off the street and they kidnapped them from people's backyards. They didn't care where they got the dogs, so long as they kept up a steady supply for their boss.

That night Vernon and Harvey were getting the Dandy Pup Pet Supply van ready to go out into Vista Valley to look for more dogs. It was thundering and raining outside, which was good for the dog-nappers. There wouldn't be many people out, and the stray dogs would be easy to lure into the trap with some food. Not even stray dogs like to be out on a cold, rainy night.

The van roared out of the warehouse into the dark streets. Vernon was driving. He was a thin, dark-haired, sort of greasy-looking guy who needed a shave. He seemed to be always in a bad mood. Harvey was a lot heavier than his partner, with curly hair and a fixed, kind of stupid look on his face. He had a tendency to be afraid of everything, which made him a not really successful criminal.

Vernon and Harvey cruised the dirty streets around the Dandy Pup warehouse looking for strays. They found a couple near the sewage-treatment plant. One was an old mutt who seemed to be happy to get out of the rain — until he was thrust into a cage in the back of the van. The shabby old dog knew instantly that he was in danger, cowering in the corner of his dirty cage. The other catch was a little Jack Russell terrier. He wore a collar with his name on it — Sparky — and he took one look at Vernon and Harvey and the cages in the back of the van, and knew he would have to escape — fast.

They drove up and down the streets for a couple of hours and they only nabbed those two dogs. Vernon and Harvey were getting fed up, but they knew that they couldn't go back to the warehouse with only two dogs to show for a night's work.

'The doc's gonna be real mad at us,' said Harvey.

'That's a brilliant observation,' said Vernon sourly.

'He'll have our hides. Gonna be real angry. Probably fire us. Or worse.'

Vernon slammed the steering-wheel with the heels of his hands, pounding angrily. 'Would you be quiet, please? I'm trying to think here.'

'What are you thinking about?'

'I'm thinking about where we can get some fresh dogs. Puppies.'

'Puppies would be good,' agreed Harvey. He was silent for a long time as he tried to figure out where puppies came from. Finally he said, 'Where we gonna get puppies from, Vernon?'

'From a pet shop.'

'A pet shop? I think they're all closed by now, Vern. Besides, wouldn't that cost a lot of money?'

'Don't be an ignoramus. We're gonna *steal* 'em.'

'Oh. Good thinking.'

The dogs in the Land-O-Pets shop were not having a very good night. The puppies were all afraid of the thunder and lightning that was booming and flashing. The little St Bernard puppy was waiting anxiously for the morning light and the return of the nice girls who gave him food, not to mention the people on the street who made such a fuss over him.

He looked out of the window at the rainy, deserted street. Morning seemed a year away. But just then, Vernon and Harvey arrived in their van. The St Bernard jumped up on his hind legs, his tail wagging as he saw the two men getting out.

Vernon and Harvey stood looking at the pet shop, each with a big sack in his hand.

'That's it,' said Vernon.

'And we're gonna break in?' asked Harvey.

'That's right.'

'Well, in that case,' said Harvey, 'we should have a disguise.'

'A disguise?'

Harvey pulled two neon-orange ski-hats from his pocket, both with little bobbles on top, and showed them to his partner. 'Don't say no right away,' he said. 'Give yourself a minute to get used to the idea.'

'No way!' growled Vernon. He grabbed the two ski-hats from Harvey's hand and tossed them in the back of the van. 'Get serious!' he ordered.

Harvey looked hurt. He thought it had been a pretty good idea.

Vernon led the way to the front door of the pet shop. 'You don't need a disguise. I cased the place and it's a pushover! Now, come on.' He lit a cigarette and puffed on it heavily.

'Is now the time for a smoke?' asked Harvey.

'Shut up.' Vernon looked up and down the deserted pavement and then leaned against the flimsy front door of the pet shop, his elbow resting on one pane of glass in the entrance.

'What about the alarm?' asked Harvey in a panicked whisper.

Very quickly, Vernon slammed his elbow through the glass and reached in through the jagged hole and undid the lock. He took a deep drag on his cigarette and blew it through the doorway. The smoke swirled and got caught in a tiny beam of light that stretched across the entrance. It was an infra-red alarm beam.

'That's the alarm,' he whispered. 'All you gotta do is step over it.'

'Got it,' said Harvey, starting to go into the shop. Vernon grabbed him by the shoulder and yanked him back. 'But don't step on the doormat. It's wired with an alarm too!'

'Ooops,' said Harvey.

Together the thieves stepped over the alarm, taking care to avoid the doormat. Vernon closed the door behind them and grinned. All the dogs were looking at the two intruders curiously, wondering what was going to happen next.

'What did I tell you?' Vernon muttered. 'In and out, as quiet as a mouse.'

'You are one smart guy, Vern,' said Harvey admiringly.

Then, all of a sudden, every dog in the pet shop started to howl at the tops of their voices. The St Bernard was the loudest!

Harvey almost leapt out of his skin when the racket started. He jumped back in fright, covering his ears. And then he stepped on the doormat! In an instant, the alarm sounded. The siren wailed, lights flashed and bells rang. The dogs howled and yelped and barked. Suddenly there was enough noise coming out of the pet shop to wake up the whole town.

'Get some dogs! Get 'em now!' Vernon ordered.

The two thieves immediately started opening the cages, grabbing the dogs by the scruff of the neck and stuffing them into the sacks. The instant the St Bernard got shoved down into the sack, he popped out and scampered across the pet shop and out of the front door. Getting crammed into a dark, smelly sack was not for him!

Vernon and Harvey swung the wriggling sacks over their shoulders and ran for it. The St Bernard was still on the pavement and Vernon grabbed him and threw him in the sack.

'C'mon!' shouted Harvey. 'Hurry!'

Police sirens could be heard in the distance.

The two dog-nappers jumped into the van. Vernon started the engine and they zoomed away. Harvey

11

stayed in the back, roughly grabbing the dogs out of the sacks and throwing them into the cages.

The little St Bernard was terrified!

Sparky, the stray they had picked up earlier that night, barked at him, shouting encouragement. 'Don't give up,' he said. 'We'll get out of here!'

When Harvey had finished, he climbed into the front seat of the van. It was travelling very fast, zooming through the deserted streets.

Vernon checked the rear-view mirror, looking for the police. They didn't seem to be following. He smiled, pleased with himself.

'Now,' he shouted at Harvey, 'don't this beat taking strays off the street?'

'You're right! You are a genius!'

'Don't you ever forget it.'

'Don't worry, I won't.' Harvey clapped his partner in crime on the shoulder. But jostling him like that made the van swerve, the front wheel jumping the kerb and bumping hard.

'Watch it!'

Vernon got the van back under control in a second.

'Don't do that again,' he ordered.

'Sorry,' said Harvey.

But the damage had been done. When the van had hit the kerb, the force of the bump had upset one of the cages in the back of the van. Sparky's cage had crashed down and the rusty catch had broken open. The cage was wedged in the tight little corridor between the two rows of cells. That didn't matter to Sparky. Quick as a flash, he darted out of his cage.

The little St Bernard pup saw that his new friend was free and started barking wildly, which seemed to set all the other dogs off.

Sparky jumped up and pawed at the catch of the St Bernard's cage. The latch wasn't fastened very tight, so it popped open. The St Bernard jumped to the floor and watched as Sparky leapt in the air, trying to get the back door of the van open. All the other dogs barked and howled, shouting their encouragement.

Vernon slowed the vehicle down a little. He cocked his head, listening to the racket in the back of the van.

'Why are they barking?'

Harvey thought for a moment. 'Because they're dogs?'

'Go back and check, Harvey,' Vernon ordered.

'"Go back and check, Harvey. Go back and check, Harvey." Why is it always me that's gotta go back and check?'

''CAUSE I'M DRIVING!' Vernon shouted angrily.

That seemed to make sense to Harvey. 'Oh. Right. Good point.' He swung out of his seat and made his way into the back of the van. He was shocked by what he saw.

Sparky had managed to open the back door of the van, and the instant Harvey appeared, he and the St Bernard pup jumped into the street.

'Oh no!' yelled Harvey. 'Vernon! Stop the van!'

Vernon stamped on the brakes and the van skidded to a halt in the wet street.

Sparky and the St Bernard were not going to hang around to see what happened next. The two dogs took off, each going in a different direction. Sparky was the older dog, more streetwise and a lot faster than his young friend. He ran as fast as he could down the street and soon vanished from sight.

The little St Bernard puppy was terrified. He darted into an old dustbin that was lying on the pavement. He tried to make himself as tiny as possible, curling into a tight little ball, cowering in fear. He heard the sound of angry voices and he knew that if the men found him, they would certainly hurt him. He wondered where his friend Sparky was and hoped that he had managed to get away. The little puppy felt very lonely.

Vernon was stomping around the street, shouting and cursing, yelling at Harvey.

'That was really smart! Why did you open the door? If we had lost all the dogs, then the boss would have killed us. I don't know how you're going to talk your way out of this one.'

'I didn't open the door. The dog did it!' protested Harvey.

'The dog did it?' Vernon folded his arms across his chest and looked at Harvey as if he was crazy.

'That's right,' insisted Harvey. 'The dog opened the door all by himself.'

'What? Are you saying a dog is smarter than you?'

'Well . . .'

Vernon slammed the van door, catching Harvey's finger.

'Owwww!' He jammed his finger into his stomach, cradling it. 'You did that on purpose!'

'That's right,' said Vernon as he climbed back behind the wheel of the van.

'You're sadistic!'

'Right again.' He slammed the van into gear and sped off into the night.

CHAPTER THREE

The thunderstorm of the night before had cleared the air, and the rain had washed the streets of Vista Valley. It looked like it was going to be a great morning in the peaceful little town. Slowly, the town came to life. By the time the sun was up, there were joggers in the square, the newspaper boys and girls were collecting copies of the *Vista Valley Gazette* from the printing plant, shops were opening up and the rubbish trucks were grinding through the streets, making their early-morning rounds.

The little St Bernard pup was still in his dustbin, fast asleep, his head on his big white paws. As the rubbish truck approached, the growling of the engine woke him up, and he stirred and yawned and stretched. For a moment he couldn't quite remember where he was or what had happened to him. Then it all came flooding back.

As the rubbish truck bore down on him, he scooted out of his makeshift shelter and darted down the street. The St Bernard trotted down the pavement, his eyes wide with wonder. He looked at the houses, the trees and shrubs, the big cars parked in the driveways and the green lawns and felt a little jolt of excitement. This was the outside world!

The world he had watched day after day from the pet-shop window, the world he had longed to join. He was thrilled to be out in the great big wide world, but he also felt a little anxious. He was alone and he was hungry and he didn't know the first thing about living in the real world.

There were scary things out here too. Like the paper-boy on his red bike who almost ran him down as he crossed the street, or the car that came blazing along the same road. The dog scampered away from those two close shaves, darting under a hedge to hide from these terrible, frightening things.

After a few minutes, the natural curiosity of the little dog got the better of him and he ventured out from his hiding-place to take a closer look at his new surroundings. He ambled down the pavement, enjoying the fresh air and the smell of the grass and flowers. The sun was warm and the birds were chirping and the world seemed, on the whole, a pretty good place to be. The puppy had the feeling that he was going to be very happy here.

Of course, he knew enough about life to know that he had to find a family to live with, a family with lots of kids he could play with and love. He crossed the street and looked at a house on the corner. It was a neat little house, a nice place to live. There was a bike lying in the driveway and toys scattered here and there on the front lawn – that told him that this family had children of the right age. He made his way towards the path that led up to the house, all the while looking at it and telling himself that *this* was the place he was going to live in. Not bad . . .

Except there was a rude surprise waiting for him on the other side of the neat picket fence that encircled the property. As he struggled under the gate, he came face to face with his first cat, a big, fluffy Persian. She was sunning herself on the path, enjoying the warmth and peace of the morning. She was *not* in the mood to have her lazy morning interrupted by a rowdy puppy. The St Bernard would have been happy to make friends with this strange-looking creature, but the cat wanted nothing to do with him. The instant she saw him, she reared up, her back arched, her fur standing on end. Her claws were out like sharp knives and she spat and hissed, showing her pointed teeth. The pup definitely got the feeling he was not welcome!

He dashed back out on the pavement as fast as his stumpy little legs would carry him. The cat had scared him, and as he ran down the street, he felt his small heart beating in his chest. Not everybody was nice in the big wide world, he told himself. He would have to be very careful.

But the world was so interesting! It was full of sights and scenes and smells that he had never experienced before. On the front lawn of one of the houses stood a man with a leaf-blower, a big, noisy machine that shot a stream of air over the debris lying on the grass, driving it into a big heap. The pup found this roaring machine absolutely fascinating. Carefully, he approached to take a closer look. But just as he did so, the man with the leaf-blower turned and sent a blast of air in the direction of the puppy. It was like being caught in a great storm. The shot of air blew him head over heels and the little St Bernard thought it might be better if he went and explored something else.

He scurried down the pavement to the next house. The pup sat down on the path and took in the scene before him. The house was charming. A perfect-looking place with a nice lawn and porch, rose bushes and shrubs and a big oak tree shading the front garden. There were some bikes in the driveway and a little red wagon – sure signs of children.

But, best of all, there was a man standing on the front step of the porch. A very nice-looking man, a man with a kind face and as tidy-looking as his house. The pup decided he *liked* him. He decided he would live here.

The man didn't notice the tiny dog; he was looking down the street, as if waiting for something. He was waiting for the paper-boy, the one who had almost run down the puppy a few streets away. The man glanced at his watch.

'Seven o'clock,' he said aloud. 'Where is that newspaper?'

As if the paper-boy had heard him, he came zooming down the street on his bike and launched the newspaper as he whizzed by. The newspaper flew through the air and hit the ground, pages scattering all over the grass.

'Hey!' shouted the man. 'Get it right next time!' Grumbling to himself, he started picking up the pieces of the newspaper, putting it back together again.

Once it was all assembled, he looked at the front page. He didn't pay much attention to the headline – 'Mysterious Break-in at Land-O-Pets' – because it had nothing to do with him. He turned to the business pages and was immediately engrossed in the dry text.

The little St Bernard puppy darted through the man's legs, up the porch steps and into the house. He dashed into the carpeted hall and ran for the steep staircase, clambering up the steps towards the second floor. The climb was hard for the little dog. He had to put his forepaws on the stair and pull himself up, his hind legs pushing his little rump up and over.

Mr George Newton was a tidy, orderly, organized man who lived by the motto: 'A place for everything and everything in its place'. He followed an unvarying routine and expected the world to be as neat and efficient as he was. In this he was often disappointed, but he could be sure of one thing, that his house and family would always run like clockwork.

He finished his quick look at the business page, tucked the newspaper under his arm and walked into the house. He didn't see the dog, who had already made it to the top.

Mr Newton stood in the middle of the hall and consulted his wristwatch again.

'Hey!' he shouted. 'It's past seven o'clock. Up and at 'em. Rise and shine!'

The puppy was standing in the doorway of the master bedroom, watching the effect of Mr Newton's words.

Alice Newton, Mr Newton's wife, groaned and rolled over. She was half asleep, but she struggled to sit up in the bed. She picked up the alarm clock on the bedside table and squinted at it. The puppy looked at Mrs Newton and decided he liked her too. She was blonde and pretty and a few years younger than her husband. She also appeared to be a little more relaxed, more likely to take things in her stride.

'Morning, Mom,' said a small voice.

Alice Newton rolled to the edge of the bed and peered down at the floor. Stretched out next to the bed, wrapped in a blanket, was her eight-year-old son, Ted. He was a slight, frail boy with a sweet, endearing look to him.

'Hi, honey,' said Mrs Newton. 'What are you doing there? Nightmares again?'

Ted nodded matter of factly. 'Yeah.'

'Poor baby.' Mrs Newton ruffled Ted's brown hair gently, then swung out of bed, ready to face the day.

Her son wasn't so sure. He slipped on a pair of big, owlish, horn-rimmed glasses which dwarfed his tiny face and looked at the digital watch on his thin wrist.

'It's Saturday, Mom, and it's 7.02. Do we really have to get up already?'

Mrs Newton sighed. She wouldn't have minded a few more minutes in bed herself. 'You heard your father,' she said. 'Rise and shine.'

'I can handle the rise,' said Ted. 'It's the shine I'm not so sure about.'

The puppy hurried down the hall to get a look at the other members of the family. The next door he came to was plastered with posters — Hammer, Bon Jovi — and a stern warning: No Trespassing! Trespassers Will Be Shot!

The door opened and out stepped a very sleepy Ryce Newton, Alice and George's oldest child. She was thirteen years old, tall and blonde with lanky long legs that seemed to have grown a little faster than the rest of her. She was rubbing her eyes and did not look very happy about being so rudely awakened.

'Mom,' she called, 'I have a newsflash for you. It's Saturday.'

Mrs Newton came out of her room, Ted following. 'I know, honey.'

'Why do we have to get up so early?' grumbled Ryce.

'Ask your father.'

The puppy nosed open the last bedroom door on the second floor and, with all his might, jumped up on the bed. A little girl was sound asleep there, blissfully unaware that her father had commanded that the family rise and shine. Emily Newton was five years old, with long, curly, brown hair and blue eyes. The puppy looked at her a moment, then fell on her, licking her plump cheeks. Emily stirred, opened her eyes and sat bolt upright in the bed.

'Mommy! Mommy!'

Mrs Newton came rushing into the room, Ryce and Ted right behind her.

'Mommy!' shouted Emily in delight. 'Look! I had a dream and it came true! I dreamed we had a puppy! And here he is!'

Ryce and Ted immediately threw themselves on the bed and started stroking the puppy.

'Wow!' exclaimed Ted.

'He's so cute!' cried Ryce

All Mrs Newton could do was stare.

CHAPTER FOUR

Mr Newton was enjoying a peaceful breakfast when his whole family came bursting into the kitchen. Emily clutched the puppy in her arms like a trophy.

Alice Newton gave her husband a big kiss on the cheek, almost making him spill his coffee on his spotless white shirt.

'George, darling! I take back everything I ever said about your being cold and insensitive!'

George didn't understand what his wife was talking about. 'Why?'

Ryce gave her father a hug. 'Dad, I take back anything *I* ever said about you too.'

'Why?'

Ted slapped his father on the back. 'Dad, I have everything I ever wanted. I owe you big time.'

'You too? What's going on?'

Emily thrust the puppy into Mr Newton's face. 'Daddy, can we call him Fred?'

The puppy licked Mr Newton's face enthusiastically and barked a happy bark. He was home at last!

'Let's take him outside!' yelled Emily. The three Newton children ran out of the kitchen door, giggling happily.

Mrs Newton stayed behind with her husband. George looked shellshocked and horrified. There was *no way* a dog could fit into the Newton family scheme of things.

'There has been a terrible mistake,' he managed to stammer. 'I didn't have anything to do with getting that dog. It must be a stray. I'll have to take it down to the pound.'

'You can't show a child a puppy and take it away two minutes later,' said Mrs Newton.

George got up and paced the kitchen nervously. 'I didn't show a child a puppy. It is obviously lost. If you can occupy the kids, I'll get hold of it and drive it down to the humane society.'

'But, George,' protested Alice, 'if the owner doesn't claim him, he might be destroyed.'

'If we keep him, our *house* will be destroyed,' insisted her husband.

Alice Newton was pretty good in the common-sense department. 'Honey, it's a dog. Millions of people have dogs.'

'Not people like me. Dogs lick, they sniff, they chew, they wet, they shed, they drool, they dig, they whine.' He thought for a moment, trying to think of other terrible dog habits. 'They have *parasites*,' he said, with a shiver of horror.

Gales of laughter from the Newton children floated in through the open kitchen window. Alice looked out at them playing with the puppy.

'But, George . . . They love it so much already.'

'They'll lose interest. I'll have to look after it, it'll grow to be enormous and take over the yard, the bushes will die, the lawn will look terrible, and when the dog finally settles down, it will die and everybody will be so upset, we'll have to go and get another puppy and the whole thing will start all over again. Do you understand?'

'Could you be more specific?' deadpanned Alice.

'I could use a little support here, honey. You have to back me up.'

Alice Newton sighed. 'I'm sorry. How should we handle this?'

'This is how I think we should handle it . . .'

'Yes?'

'*You* go tell the kids we can't keep the dog.'

'Do your own dirty work, George,' said Mrs Newton. 'Because I'm not going to do it for you.'

'But honey, they'll hate me . . .'

'Better you than me.'

'Thanks a lot.' He squared his shoulders and headed for the kitchen door. 'You know, deep down, I'm right. It might look like I'm being cruel now, but you'll thank me for this. You'll see.'

Mrs Newton did not look convinced.

Little Emily was sitting on the grass, the puppy on her lap. It gave her a big wet kiss and jumped up, pushing her over. She tumbled, laughing, on to the grass.

Ted ran past, and the puppy took off after him, barking and yipping at the top of his voice. Ryce threw a big blue rubber ball and the puppy went for it, falling over himself trying to get the ball in his tiny jaws. All three kids looked so happy. Even George Newton had to admit it was a cute scene.

He thrust his hands in his pockets. 'Hi, kids.'

'Hi, Dad!' they answered.

'Look,' said Ryce, pointing at the puppy, who was still wrestling with the ball. 'He already knows how to fetch, sort of.'

The puppy gave up his tussle with the ball and ran over to Mr Newton and started tugging his shoelaces. 'Hey, now. Stop that. Get lost.' He tried to shoo away the puppy, who looked up at him, puzzlement in his eyes. Why didn't the big man want to play? Everybody else did!

'Daddy,' asked Emily. 'Can he sleep in my room?'

'He's sleeping in *my* room,' insisted Ted.

'Dream on!' said Ryce. 'I'm the oldest. He's sleeping in my room.'

'He's not sleeping in anyone's room,' said George Newton. 'Now listen to me for a minute, OK?'

The kids quietened down and stopped playing with the puppy. Even the little dog seemed to be paying attention.

George Newton took a deep breath. 'As you know, we are not dog people . . .'

'Yes we are!' insisted Ryce.

'Let me finish. We aren't dog people. We're people people. We're goldfish people. We are ant-farm people . . .'

'You can't teach an ant to fetch,' observed Ted. 'Can't do it with a goldfish either.'

'You kids have no idea what it means to have a dog. It's not all "Here, boy, fetch" and laughing . . .'

The Newton children exchanged looks. *Oh, no,*

they were thinking, *here it comes.* They must have been crazy to think that their dad would actually let them keep a dog. Their faces started to crumple in disappointment.

'There's a lot of work involved in having a dog. You have to walk a dog each and every day.'

'I'll walk him!' cried Ted.

'I'll help,' said Emily. 'I promise, Daddy.'

It was really tearing George up to break his children's hearts like this. But there was nothing else he could do.

'Who's going to feed him? You have to feed him. Every day. Morning and night.'

Ted volunteered. 'I'll feed him, Dad. Scouts' honour.'

'You say that now, but later you'll forget. And you know who would have to do all the work? Mom and me, that's who.'

'Give us a chance!' shouted Ryce. 'We need to learn how to handle responsibility! That's what you keep on saying!'

George could not let himself be dissuaded. He pressed on, trying to make his children see reason. 'We have a nice, new house here. A house that your mother and I have invested a lot of time, money and effort in.'

Emily put out her arms and hugged the puppy, sniffing back a tear. George Newton felt as if someone had plunged a dagger into his heart.

'I knew it,' said Ryce in disgust.

'Yup,' said Ted. 'Business as usual.'

Emily was sobbing now and Mrs Newton went to comfort her, shooting a nasty glance over her shoulder at her husband.

George cleared his throat. 'Therefore, your mother and I have decided . . .'

'A-*hem*,' corrected Alice.

George quickly changed what he was going to say. The whole family was staring at him accusingly.

'My sole decision . . . It's my decision . . .' The puppy was very distressed by Emily's tears. He started whimpering and pawing at her, trying to make her feel better.

'My mind is made up,' said George. 'I . . . I . . .' He took a deep breath. 'You kids had better give him a name so that I have something to yell at him when he tears up the house.'

The three children looked at him. Suddenly, Emily wasn't crying any more.

'You mean . . .?' stammered Ted.

'You mean we can keep him?' yelled Ryce.

'Just until we find the owners,' said George.

'Yay!' screamed the three Newton kids. They fell on their father and hugged him.

Mrs Newton's eyes filled with tears of happiness. She knew that her husband wasn't the old meany he pretended to be. She hoped that the children realized it now too.

The St Bernard certainly understood. He capered around the family, jumping up against the children's legs and barking frantically. He finally had a home to call his own!

CHAPTER FIVE

The first thing the Newtons had to do with the new member of their family was to give him a name. Mr and Mrs Newton, Ryce, Ted and Emily all had different opinions on this subject and they argued about it for hours. Each of them had their own favourite name for the puppy. At the rate they were going, it looked like the dog would never get a name. The whole family was becoming tired of the debate and wished it were over, but no one would give in and agree to someone else's choice.

Emily was the first to get tired of the quarrel. She plonked herself down in front of the piano and hit the keys. The puppy sat on the piano bench next to her.

'I wish we could ask *him* what name he wanted,' she said wistfully. 'He should have a say in his own name.'

The dog barked enthusiastically, as if agreeing with every word she said. She put her fingers on the piano keys and picked out a tune. No one was quite sure what she was playing, but it *could* have been 'Mary Had a Little Lamb'.

'I know what we should do,' said Mr Newton. 'We'll all write our choice of names on slips of paper, put them in a hat, and whichever one comes out first — that's his name. No arguments.'

'That sounds like a good plan,' said Mrs Newton.

'It's fair,' agreed Ted.

Ryce hurried away to get a pad and paper and some pens, pencils and crayons. There was silence for a long time as they all wrote out their choices for names, folded their slips of paper tightly and placed them in one of Ted's baseball caps.

It was agreed that Mrs Newton would pull the names from the hat.

'Remember,' cautioned Mr Newton, 'no arguments.'

Mrs Newton closed her eyes and dipped her hand into the hat. She rooted around for a moment or two and then pulled out a piece of paper. She unfolded it and read, a frown crossing her face.

'What is it?' asked Ryce.

Ted could scarcely contain his excitement. 'Yeah, what's his name going to be?'

'You can't change it, Mom. Those are the rules.'

Alice Newton showed the piece of paper to her husband. 'Well,' said George, 'it's not going to be that.'

'Emily,' asked Alice, 'did you do your name in crayon?'

'Uh-huh,' said Emily.

'Words for body-parts don't really make very good names for dogs, sweetheart.'

'No?' Emily was playing the same three notes on the piano over and over again.

'No. You see, Daddy can't stand on the back porch at night, calling the dog by that name.'

'Oh. OK.'

Alice extracted another name from the hat. 'The dog will be named . . .' She unfolded the piece of paper. 'The Hound from Hell? Let me guess, George, this was *your* contribution, wasn't it?'

'You asked for my input,' said Mr Newton.

'Well,' said Ryce indignantly, 'we are *not* calling our dog the Hound from Hell.'

'How about the Hound from Heck?' suggested Mr Newton.

'Forget about it.'

George rubbed his temples as if he were getting a headache. 'Emily, why don't you play Chopsticks for a while? I think it would be more soothing.'

Emily ignored her father. She didn't know how to play Chopsticks.

'How about Hammer?' suggested Ryce.

'No,' said Alice.

'The Ultimate Warrior?'

The puppy whimpered. He didn't like any of these names one little bit.

'He's not happy about these names, Mom,' said Emily.

'Oh, right,' snapped Ryce, 'as if you can read a dog's mind.'

'Maybe she can,' said Mrs Newton. 'Emily . . . what does he want to be called?'

'Oh, for heaven's sake,' said Mr Newton. He was irritated with the whole thing. Maybe it would be better to get rid of the dog after all. He stood up. 'This is ridiculous! He's a dog. He doesn't have preferences. You could call him Ding Dong Head and he wouldn't know the difference.'

'Yes he would,' insisted Emily. 'He'll tell us what he wants his name to be.'

The puppy looked at her and wagged his tail. Emily played the three notes again. Dum-dum-dum.

Just then the puppy barked, but he barked perfectly in key, completing the musical phrase Emily had tapped out. There was silence for a moment. Everybody stared at the dog.

'What is that piece of music?' asked Ted.

'It's the beginning of the Fifth Symphony,' said George.

Just to make sure, Emily repeated the tune and once again the little pup barked in key, his tail wagging.

'Who wrote it?' asked Ted.

'Beethoven,' whispered George Newton, not quite able to believe what he'd heard.

Emily grinned. 'See? He knows what his name should be!' She threw her arms around the little dog's neck and kissed him. 'I love you, Beethoven!'

CHAPTER SIX

To say that the Newton family changed a little bit over the next few months would be putting it mildly. The puppy, now christened Beethoven, started off small, but with a giant appetite. Every day the three Newton children fed Beethoven, three times a day. Then he started to grow ... and grow ... and grow!

Beethoven's size wasn't the only thing that changed. Slowly, but surely, the perfect Newton house came to be a little less perfect. The first thing to go was the neat little fence in the front garden. One day Beethoven tried to jump over it. He didn't quite make it and – bang! – down came a section of the fence.

As Beethoven's teeth grew, he needed to exercise them. Ted, Ryce and Emily tried to keep him supplied with dog bones, but sometimes they forgot, or sometimes Beethoven thought he would like to try something a little different. Therefore Mr Newton's collection of expensive leather shoes started disappearing into Beethoven's growing jaws.

The no-dog-in-the-car rule was one of the first to fall. Beethoven loved his new family so much that he couldn't stand to be separated from them. As soon as they headed for the car, their loving pet was right there in the back seat. Naturally, the inside of the car ended up being slightly the worse for wear. But a little slobber and chewed-up car seats never really hurt anybody.

The Newtons' neighbours came to love Beethoven just as much as his family did . . . unless Beethoven happened to get into the shrubbery, dig up the flower-beds or scatter piles of carefully raked leaves. Mr Newton got a little tired of apologizing for his dog's misdeeds. Once in a while he would rant and rave and declare that Beethoven must go!

Ryce, Ted and Emily got pretty good at making excuses for Beethoven.

'Aww, Dad, he didn't *mean* to do it,' was a popular one.

'We'll make sure *it never happens again!*' was also pretty effective.

'It wasn't his fault,' wasn't received so well because Mr Newton could always shoot back with: 'Well, who's fault was it? *Yours?*'

If all else failed, George Newton's children would look at him with their big sad blue eyes and Beethoven would look at him with his big sad brown eyes, and they would all look so miserable together that Mr Newton would have to give in and allow the dog to stay.

Sometimes Beethoven did such naughty things that even the Newton children thought they wouldn't be able to get him off the hook. When Beethoven was six months old, at Thanksgiving, he *really* got into trouble. While the children of the family were in the dining-room, eating their dinner with their parents and grandparents, Beethoven was in the kitchen, eating all the pumpkin pies.

Luckily this time Beethoven was rescued by Grandma Newton – she loved Beethoven almost as much as the children did – who declared that she had baked the pies and she could decide who would eat them. Ryce, Ted and Emily didn't mind giving up dessert if it meant saving their beloved pet. And Mr Newton couldn't argue with *his* mother, so Beethoven was spared.

A month later, though, Beethoven ate the Christmas tree and Mr Newton changed his plan. He decided that he would take Beethoven to dog-obedience school. Beethoven enjoyed meeting the other dogs in his class, but he didn't take to the lessons too well. When the instructor said 'Sit!' Beethoven stood up on his hind legs. When the teacher said 'Heel!' Beethoven sat. After a while, Mr Newton stopped taking him because it was kind of embarrassing to have Beethoven be the first dog in history to flunk out of obedience school.

Mr Newton never gave up trying to find Beethoven's real owners. Every couple of weeks he made up a set of posters with Beethoven's picture on them and walked all over town, stapling them to telegraph poles and trees. Then he would rush home and wait for the real owners to call. But no one ever did. Gradually, the posters faded in the sun or were washed out in the rain or blew away in the wind. In time, Mr Newton came to recognize that he and his family were Beethoven's true owners. It was meant to be.

Not all that Beethoven did was destructive. He remained a good sport about everything and looked very cute and funny when he was dressed up as Santa Claus at Christmas and the Easter Bunny at Easter. He didn't even mind when they put him in a clown suit for Emily's birthday party. Once, at Hallowe'en, Emily decided that she would wear a cowgirl costume. Mrs Newton made Beethoven a saddle and he went as Emily's horse!

By the next spring, Beethoven had discovered that he loved the game of golf. There was a golf course near the Newtons' home and Beethoven loved to go over there and wait in the trees until a golf ball came out of the sky and landed on the green. Then he would leap to his feet and dash out, grab the ball and run off, chased by the golfers. Beethoven knew that the men on the golf course loved the game as much as he did.

Beethoven never outgrew his passion for chewing things. As he grew older, the things he chewed on grew larger. He chomped on furniture, rugs and shrubbery. Then he moved up and crunched kitchen chairs, table legs and armchairs. A couple of times he tried to chew on metal objects – bicycles, lawn furniture and even a washing-machine. Metal was not as much fun as wood, though, so he quickly changed back to eating baseball bats, small logs, a couple of kitchen doors, window-frames and piano legs.

All the while, Beethoven continued to eat. He ate dry food that came in fifty-pound sacks and dog food that came in six-pound cans. He also consumed a great deal of garbage, table scraps, dog biscuits and bones. Naturally there were results from all this eating. Beethoven went from ten pounds, to twenty, then thirty — then fifty. Then a hundred! Finally he was fully grown at one hundred and eighty-five pounds! He weighed more than Mr Newton and more than Ryce, Ted and Emily put together. When he stood on his hind legs, he could put his paws on Mr Newton's shoulders — and Mr Newton was over six feet tall.

In a year, Beethoven went from being a cute little puppy with a high-pitched bark to a great big cute fully grown dog with a voice as deep as a cannon. He slobbered about two gallons of drool daily. He was white with a light-brown back, a black head and muzzle, with a wet black nose. His big shaggy tail wagged like a whip when he was happy and drooped sadly when he was unhappy — like when Mr Newton lost his temper and shouted and shouted till he was bright red in the face.

Beethoven may have grown to be a giant, but he never lost the loving playfulness of the puppy he had been a few short months before. Ted, Emily and Ryce could hardly remember the 'perfect' life they'd lived before Beethoven. True, the house was a disaster area, but they liked it better now. Beethoven was the best friend any of them had ever had.

CHAPTER SEVEN

It was the usual weekday breakfast scene at the Newton house. Mrs Newton was busy cooking bacon and eggs and doling out cereal and getting the younger children ready for school. Beethoven had retrieved the mail from the slot in the front hall and deposited it on the kitchen table.

George Newton was talking excitedly about the people who were going to invest in his small business, Newton Air Freshener.

'See,' he said animatedly, 'my investors said they were interested in putting twenty-five thousand dollars into the business, but I said that doesn't do me any good. If this thing is going to take off we need some *capital*, not a Band-aid.' Few things in the world excited Mr Newton as much as the air-freshener industry. It was a subject that bored the Newton kids to tears.

Beethoven wasn't crazy about it either. He nudged Mr Newton in the ribs, trying to get him to change the subject. George ignored him and kept on talking.

'... So, they say what kind of figures are we talking about and I say, well, a hundred and fifty sounds like a pretty nice neighbourhood to me ...'

Mrs Newton flipped over two slices of bacon in

the hot frying-pan. She looked a little concerned. She wasn't sure that her husband needed to expand his business, and she certainly didn't like the idea of people they didn't know investing a hundred and fifty thousand dollars in it. 'Did you really? Is that wise? When people put that kind of money into a business, they tend to think it belongs to them.'

'I don't think that's a problem, honey. And we need that kind of money. This is a business, not a tea social . . .'

Beethoven was *very* bored with all this talk of high finance. He tried to get his head under George Newton's hand, to get him to pet him. And to get him to stop talking. George ignored his dog.

But Emily didn't. She tugged at the sleeve of her father's perfect white shirt. 'Daddy?'

'What?'

'Beethoven wants you to scratch his head.'

'But I don't *want* to scratch his head.'

'But he *wants* you to.'

George looked at Beethoven as he drooled a little on the kitchen floor. 'Well, Emily, that's a lesson of life. You don't always get what you want.'

He turned back to his wife. 'I'm telling you, Alice, if I don't get this deal, I'm going to kill myself.'

'Don't talk that way, George.'

Now it was Ryce's turn to tug at her father's perfect shirt-sleeve. 'Daddy?'

'What?'

Ryce winced. 'Never mind. Forget it.'

Alice shot a sharp look at her husband. 'Kids,

leave your father alone. He has a very important day today.'

'He has an important day *every* day,' grumbled Ryce.

Beethoven woofed quietly, as if agreeing with her. Mr Newton glared at the dog. 'Now my *dog* has opinions!' Beethoven skulked into a corner. He hated it when Mr Newton was mad at him — which was most of the time.

'You see,' Mr Newton continued, 'I just know if I can get them to smell my air fresheners, I've got it made. I mean, air fresheners are very personal things. Either you love 'em or you hate 'em.'

'Dad?' ventured Ted.

'What *is* it?'

'Can I have karate lessons?'

'Why do you want to have karate lessons?'

Ted had very good reasons for wanting to learn martial arts, but he didn't want to tell his parents.

'Well . . . Brenda Feinberg is smaller than me and she has a green belt.' The truth was, bullies at school were picking on him and Ted had decided that he needed to know how to defend himself.

'How about we just get you the belt instead?'

No one was paying any attention to Beethoven.

The bacon Mrs Newton was frying was ready. She put it on her husband's plate and brought it over to the table, placing it in front of him.

'That looks good,' said Mr Newton.

Beethoven thought the same thing. He planted two big paws in Mr Newton's lap and lapped a piece of bacon right off the plate. It tasted so good that he left a pool of drool in Mr Newton's lap.

George jumped to his feet as if he had got an electric shock.

'OK! That's it! He's outta here!'

His wife came rushing over, dabbing at the slobber on his suit with a dishcloth.

'Oh, honey, it's all right.'

George was furious. 'It's not all right, Alice! I have dog drool on my trousers! I can't go to work and meet with the people from Vanguard Capital with dog drool on my trousers!' He stormed out of the kitchen and headed for the stairs.

'Why don't you change your trousers?' said Alice reasonably, all of the family, including Beethoven, following him.

George did his best to control his rage. 'I'm going to change my trousers, Alice. I can't *just* change my trousers, but that's OK. Don't worry about it.'

'Why can't you just change your trousers?' Mrs Newton asked.

He stopped on the stairs and glared at her, as if she didn't understand anything. 'If I change my trousers, I have to change my jacket. If I change my jacket, I have to change my shirt. If I change my shirt, I have to change my tie . . .'

'George,' said Mrs Newton, 'why don't you just change your trousers?'

Beethoven shrunk into a corner, a little ashamed of what he had done. He hadn't meant to cause so much trouble. He had no idea that getting dressed was such a complicated operation. He was glad he didn't have to bother with it.

CHAPTER EIGHT

Mr Newton changed quickly, then came downstairs fast. He was in a hurry – having to change his clothes had made him late and he was not happy about it. The Newton children were going off to school, but he barely paid any attention to their goodbyes. He had something more important to do.

The last thing he did before he left for work was to lock Beethoven in the big dog-pen that had been constructed in a corner of the yard. Beethoven had to be shut up, Mr Newton figured, because if he wasn't, he would get into all kinds of mischief.

Beethoven allowed himself to be dragged across the lawn and pushed into his big pen, and he did his best to look very unhappy about being shut up all day. The truth was, he wasn't all that worried about it, but he didn't want to make his master any angrier than he already was.

The instant Mr Newton's car had pulled out of the driveway, Beethoven looked to his left and to his right, as if checking to make sure that no one was watching. Then he wriggled under the fence, using a tunnel he had dug weeks ago. Once out of his little prison, he took a deep breath. Now, he thought to himself, what shall I do today?

*

Meet Mr Newton

Mrs Newton

Beethoven with his family (from left to right: Ted, Emily, Mrs Newton, Ryce, Mr Newton)

Beethoven with the Newtons' turkey

Relaxing in the garden

A 'paw' show

Watching TV

Goodnight, Beethoven

Newton Air Fresheners was a small factory in a light-industrial park on the edge of Vista Valley. It was an ordinary-looking building – except for a big, pink nose on the side of the factory and a neon sign above it that read: NEWTON AIR FRESHENERS – WORTH EVERY SCENT. Mr Newton had thought of that corny slogan himself.

George was in the factory, nervously escorting the two representatives of Vanguard Capital around the plant floor. He didn't much like the two people, a man and a woman named Brad and Brie – they were high-tech, trendy, fast-lane yuppies, four things that George Newton was not – but he was desperate to please them.

'See,' said George eagerly, 'most people don't realize it, but air fresheners are the twelfth fastest-growing area in all of household hygiene.'

Brie almost yawned in his face. 'Fascinating,' she drawled.

'And all of my air fresheners are built using a two-dip process that guarantees a longer smell life.' He grabbed one of the air fresheners out of a big bin full of them. It was a little piece of cardboard shaped like a leather jacket. 'Take a look at this. We feel that if we could just get the right amount of capital infusion, we could take this plant straight to the top. I don't mean just successful. I mean *dominant*.'

'What makes you think that?' asked Brad.

'We've got a unique product.' He handed them the little cardboard leather jacket. 'This one is my favourites. It's called "New Leather".'

Brad and Brie seemed genuinely to like the product George was showing them.

'It's so cute!' exclaimed Brie.

'I could use one of those in my Beemer!' said Brad.

'I could use one in *my* Beemer!' Brie chimed in.

'Beemer?' asked George.

'BMW,' explained Brad.

'Oh. Well, we feel that a *lot* of people could use one in their Beemers.'

'But I wouldn't want to hang it from the rear-view mirror,' said Brie with a grimace. 'Ugh. Tacky.'

'Oh, don't worry about that,' George hastened to assure her. 'They have Velcro on the back. You can hide them anywhere. Some people stick them under the dashboard.'

Brad nodded appreciatively. 'That's pretty clever. Bravo, Newton. Kudos.'

'Thank you.'

'May I take a closer look?' asked Brie.

'Of course.'

She took the air freshener and sniffed at it. Then she sort of sniffed the air around it. 'What is that smell?'

'Well, actually a blend of herbal essence with a hint of bayberry,' said George proudly.

'No, no. It's not bayberry.'

'I smell it too,' said Brad.

George was puzzled. 'Well, occasionally an old fragrance might linger . . .'

'No. It's . . . it's on your shoe.'

46

Very slowly, George looked down at his shoe. 'Beethoven,' he hissed.

'Huh?'

'Nothing,' said George. 'It's nothing at all. Why don't we step outside, get some fresh air?'

'We've got to be running along,' said Brad.

'Great,' said George, 'I'll walk you to your, er, Beemer.'

They walked out into the bright warm sunshine, George trying to scrape off his shoe as he walked, without letting Brie and Brad see him doing it.

'There's no question about it, George,' said Brad. 'You've built yourself something pretty impressive here.'

George was delighted and for a moment forgot about the stuff on the sole of his shoe. 'Thanks! So you're still interested?'

Brad and Brie nodded. 'Absolutely,' said the man. 'You know, George, we've smelled a lot of stuff, but I think I speak for Brie and myself when I say that there's no question that yours smells the best.'

Brie and Brad slipped into their sleek BMW. 'Let us crunch some numbers,' Brie said through the open window. 'And then we'll get back to you. Maybe we could get together later this week and talk things through.'

'That would be fine,' said George. 'Fine.'

'We're looking forward to it,' said Brad with a big smile. '*Ciao.*'

'*Ciao!*' said Brie.

'*Ciao!*' said George.

The car pulled out of the car-park, leaving George to scrape his shoe against the asphalt.

Brie called 'Ciao!' one more time, then turned to her partner. 'Well, I think we got him right where we want him,' she said with a smirk.

'Right,' agreed Brad. 'We'll be able to take over Newton Air Fresheners in no time at all.'

Brie laughed. 'Then it will be *ciao*, George – for good!'

Ryce was in the gym at school, watching the JV basketball team practice. The star centre of the team was Mark Bartel, a tall, handsome boy with a nice smile and a great hook shot. Ryce had a crush on him big time – but then, so did almost every other girl in her class. Mark was only dimly aware of Ryce's existence and it was driving her crazy. The moment the practice ended, Ryce was on her feet, ever so casually walking by him as he ambled off the basketball court.

'Hi, Mark,' she said as they passed.

Mark didn't even notice.

Ryce sighed unhappily and gathered up her books. It was so unfair! Mark didn't even know she was alive and she knew everything there was to know about him – except what it was like to have a conversation with him.

Sadly, she headed out to lunch. It wasn't just that Mark didn't know who she was. All the more annoying was that *he* had a major crush on Donna Dittsworth, the prettiest and most popular girl in the class.

Out in the playground, Ryce unwrapped her sandwich and settled under a tree, where she could have a perfect view of Donna and Mark and all the really popular kids having lunch together. She hated the torture of watching, but she would have hated *not* watching more.

The only good thing about lunch-hour was that Beethoven came ambling into the schoolyard and walked up to Ryce and licked her hand. She gave him half her sandwich, which he wolfed down appreciatively, and then he settled at her feet.

'See those kids over there, Beethoven?'

Beethoven woofed softly.

'They're the coolest kids in the school. And you see that pretty blonde girl? That's Donna Dittsworth – she's the most popular girl in the school. All the boys love her. You know why? Because she's perfect.'

Beethoven looked into Ryce's face. She looked and sounded so sad and that made him sad too. All the cool kids cracked up laughing at something Donna said and Ryce could feel her cheeks burning with envy.

'Donna tells great jokes. Her hair is so pretty. Isn't it perfect? Her teeth are perfect, too, and she hasn't got any freckles.' Ryce looked at her own lightly freckled arms. 'But that's not the worst of it. You'd think that because of all this she would be really stuck up, but she's nice. She's even nice to her little brother!'

Even Beethoven, who was nice to everybody, found this piece of information astonishing.

Ryce looked down at Beethoven, then pointed at Donna Dittsworth. 'Slime her, Beethoven! Go get her!'

Beethoven didn't move. Instead, he looked sadly at Ryce as if to say: Now you don't really mean that . . .

Ryce lowered her arm and felt ashamed of herself. 'I guess you're right.' She sighed deeply. Donna wasn't with the cool kids any more. She had finished her lunch and was heading back into the school building. 'How do you get someone to notice you when you're trying to act nonchalant?'

Now *that* was a question Beethoven could answer. He grabbed a stick that was lying on the ground and walked over to Mark Bartel.

'Wow,' said Mark, 'look at this cool dog!'

Beethoven did his best to look cool.

'You want me to throw the stick? Huh, boy?' Mark reached down to take the stick out of Beethoven's mouth, but Beethoven wouldn't let go. Instead, the instant Mark grabbed the stick, Beethoven started leading him over towards where Ryce was sitting.

Ryce gulped when she saw what was happening, and she got so nervous that the first thing she thought of doing was running away. But then she stopped herself — Beethoven had brought her this far, and she was not going to chicken out.

Beethoven delivered Mark to Ryce. It was up to her now.

'Wow,' said Mark, 'what a great dog! Is he yours?'

'Yeah,' said Ryce, patting Beethoven's head. 'He's the best!'

'He's smart too!' exclaimed Mark. 'What's his name?'

'Beethoven,' said Ryce. She never wanted this moment to end and it was all due to Beethoven.

'Hi, Beethoven!' said Mark.

Beethoven woofed happily.

The bell rang and Mark looked unhappy, like he wished that he could play with Beethoven all day.

'Well, gotta go – see ya later, Ryce.'

Ryce looked as if she were going to faint with joy. Mark knew her name! She reached down and hugged her dog. 'Thank you, Beethoven!'

Lunch had not been quite so successful for Ted. He had gone out to the picnic tables that were in the playground and settled down with a couple of his friends. Ted wasn't a nerd exactly, but he was far from the coolest kid in his class, and he always sat with kids like him – other frail-looking kids with glasses. He unwrapped his sandwich and was enjoying himself until he noticed that his companions were slipping away from the table.

'Where you going, guys?' asked Ted.

'Gotta run,' said one of his friends.

'Yup. Catch you later . . .' said the other.

Ted turned around and saw what was going on. The three bullies who lived to make Ted's life miserable were approaching. They were big kids who didn't care how much trouble they got into or how obnoxious they were. They were called Bob, Bill and Bart, but Ted had secret nicknames for all three, each name highlighting something about the three nasty kids: Crew Cut, Leather Jacket and the Brat.

Crew Cut and Leather Jacket sat down on either side of Ted and examined his lunch.

'Why, Ted,' said Leather Jacket, pretending to be friendly. 'That's a fine-looking lunch you have there.'

Ted looked at his lunch. It was a perfectly normal lunch. A sandwich, a Granola bar, some fruit.

'My lunch?' said Ted. 'D-d-do you want my lunch?'

The three offensive boys laughed as if this was the funniest thing they had ever heard.

'We wouldn't *dream* of taking your lunch,' said the Brat. 'We want you to have it. Make you grow up big and strong.'

Ted hung his head. He felt tiny, puny and weak next to these three boys.

'Why don't you leave me alone?' he asked sadly.

'We want you to make sure you eat your lunch,' said Leather Jacket. 'You have to eat this nutritious meal.'

'And don't forget to wash it down with a big glass of milk!' yelled the Brat. With that, he turned Ted's carton of milk over and drenched the sandwich until it was sodden. The three jerks got a *big* laugh out of that.

Then Crew Cut patted him on the back. 'See you later,' he said ominously. 'On the bus . . .'

Ted watched them walk away and then he looked down sadly at his ruined lunch. The bus-ride home would be agony. Why wouldn't they just leave him alone?

CHAPTER NINE

Unlike the other kids in his class, Ted didn't want the school day to end. He kept on watching the clock on the classroom wall, urging the hands backward, trying to stop time, desperately attempting to delay the inevitable.

But three o'clock came, as he knew it must. The bell rang and Ted packed up his backpack, slung it around his shoulders and plodded wearily towards the school bus. He picked a seat in the middle of the bus and hunched down, hoping that he could survive the fifteen-minute ride home.

The bus filled up gradually, and for a moment Ted allowed himself to hope that Leather Jacket, Crew Cut and the Brat wouldn't show up. But just as the door of the bus was about to hiss shut, the three bullies swaggered on, laughing and shouting as if they owned the place.

The three of them strutted down the aisle, making fun of the kids they passed. knocking off caps and snatching at glasses, and insulting everyone within earshot.

But for some reason Ted couldn't figure out, his three persecutors reserved their cruellest torments for him. *Why me?*, he wondered. What had he ever done to any of them?

Bart, Bill and Bob stood over Ted, looking as if they were really enjoying the torture they were about to inflict on their victim. Ted cowered in his seat.

'Hey, that's a nice backpack, Teddy,' said Leather Jacket as he snatched it off the seat. 'Can I see it?' He unzipped the backpack and dumped the contents on the floor of the bus, all three of the boys kicking Ted's books and belongings under the bus seats.

Ted looked around at the other kids on the bus, as if begging them to help. But they pretended not to see – all of the kids on the bus were afraid of the three bullies.

'C'mon, guys,' pleaded Ted. 'Leave me alone.' As he bent down to retrieve his stuff from the floor, Crew Cut grabbed Ted's glasses off his face and tossed them to the Brat.

'Hey! Give those back to me! Leave me alone!' Ted just plain couldn't see without his glasses. He peered at his attackers and waved his arms in front of him, trying to get hold of his glasses again.

The three bullies formed a ring around him and tossed the glasses from one to the other, keeping them just out of Ted's reach. They were laughing and giggling, shouting in delight at the pain they were inflicting on poor little Ted.

They were making so much noise that the bus driver couldn't stand it. 'Hey! You kids!' he bellowed from the front of the bus. 'Give him back his glasses!' The bullies froze in the middle of their cruel game and handed the glasses to Ted.

'Now, sit down!' ordered the bus driver.

Leather Jacket, Crew Cut and the Brat collapsed on to one of the seats. Ted stuffed his books into his backpack and prepared to get off the bus.

'Hey, Teddy,' whispered Leather Jacket.

'What?'

Leather Jacket raised his fist. 'Next stop, Teddy, next stop.'

Ted gulped.

The instant the bus stopped, Ted dashed off the bus and raced down the street towards his house. The three bullies leapt off at the same time and chased after Ted.

They were bigger and faster than Ted and they soon caught up with him, surrounding him.

'Hey, Teddy boy! Where are you going? Home to Mommy?' taunted Leather Jacket.

'Yea, what's the matter?' demanded the Brat. 'Afraid to fight?'

'You got us into trouble on the bus,' yelled Crew Cut.

Ted despaired of trying to explain to them that they got themselves into trouble.

'Chicken!' screamed the Brat.

Ted wasn't a chicken, but there were three of them and one of him. They were bigger too. There was no way he could fight them. There was only one thing he could do. Ted turned and ran.

'Teddy!' howled Leather Jacket, taking off after him.

Beethoven was asleep on the sofa in the Newton house. He heard Leather Jacket's screech and opened his eyes and sat up. He cocked his head for a moment and listened.

'Teddy!' Beethoven knew the name and he also knew the tone of voice. It was not friendly. Beethoven growled and hopped off the sofa, running for the front door.

Ted had dropped his backpack to lighten his load and was racing down the street as fast as he could, as if his life depended on it. The three kids were in hot pursuit.

'Chicken!'

'Mama's boy!'

'Coward!'

Ted wasn't any of those things. He was just a small kid who didn't think he should stand still and get beaten up by three big kids. Why couldn't they understand that?

He tore around a corner. He was close to home — a few more yards and he would be safe. But before he could reach safety, the kids were on him, forcing him up against a big green hedge. He was trapped, cornered. Ted was gasping for breath, his lungs burning, his heart pounding in his chest. Leather Jacket and his friends closed in on him. Ted accepted the inevitable. There was nothing he could do but stand and fight.

'Maybe you need your mama to walk you home, Mama's boy,' sneered Leather Jacket. He shoved Ted roughly, throwing him back into the greenery.

Ted tried to break through the wall of boys, but they caught him and threw him back again.

The Brat shook his fist under Ted's nose. 'Prepare to die, Teddy!'

Ted swallowed hard and took off his glasses, putting them in his pocket. He raised his small fists, determined to go down swinging if he had to.

Very quietly, Beethoven, in all his one hundred and eighty-five pound glory, stepped out from behind the shrubbery. His lips were curled up and he bared his sharp fangs, staring with hate-filled eyes at the three bullies.

Ted couldn't see exactly what was going on, but he sensed that the bullies had suddenly lost interest in fighting him. He had no idea that Beethoven was standing behind him, ready to attack if the boys tried to hurt Ted.

Ted took a step forward, his fists still out in front of him. Beethoven matched his step, his head slung low and mean, murder in his eyes.

The bullies had no intention of taking on Beethoven. 'Hey,' said Leather Jacket, 'what's goin' on here?'

Crew Cut backed away in fear. 'He looks really mean!'

Ted assumed they were talking about him. He advanced another step. 'Don't wanna fight now?' he yelled.

Silently, Beethoven lunged forward, his big, powerful jaws open and snapping.

'Let's get out of here!' shrieked the Brat, his voice high and tight with fear.

The bullies needed no further encouragement. They turned and ran. Beethoven smiled to himself and darted away. Mission accomplished. His friend Ted was saved.

Ted put on his glasses and enjoyed the sight of his tormentors running down the street. 'Get outta here and don't come back!' he yelled.

Ted took a deep breath, puffing his chest out with pride. He went back for his backpack and then swaggered up to his house.

CHAPTER TEN

Later that night, the Newton family was settling in for bed, and Ryce was in her room, talking to Beethoven.

She was going around and around, trying to make sense of her brief encounter with Mark that day. 'See, I know it doesn't mean that he *likes* me . . .'

Beethoven nodded in understanding.

'Do you think he *could* like me, Beethoven?'

Beethoven leaned forward and licked her face affectionately. Ryce giggled. 'Well, I know *you* like me.' Ryce gave her beloved dog a big hug and sighed.

'You're lucky you're not thirteen,' she whispered in his big furry ear. She was rewarded with another wet lick.

'I think you're gorgeous too.' She enfolded him in her arms and snuggled against him. 'Good night, Beethoven.'

Ryce's father leaned into the room. 'Good night, sweetheart,' he said. He pointed at Beethoven. 'You! Out!'

Obediently, Beethoven jumped off the bed and followed Mr Newton out of Ryce's bedroom.

George paused in the hall to knock on the bathroom door. 'Ted? Are you in there?'

'Yes, Dad.'

'Go to bed.'

'Yes, Dad.'

Ted was standing in front of the mirror in the bathroom, his shirt off. He looked at himself for a moment or two, then raised his thin arms and struck a body-builder pose, flexing his dinky muscles. He held the stance for a second, then smiled at his reflection, recalling his confrontation with the bullies. He didn't think he would have any bad dreams that night.

An hour or so later, all the Newton children were in bed asleep and George and Alice were getting ready for bed themselves. George was still glowing from the good news he had heard from Brad and Brie that day – visions of untold wealth shimmered in his brain.

He was already busy spending the money he hadn't earned yet.

'The first thing we'll do is get a great new house. In a few years we'll drive by this house and laugh.'

Alice frowned. 'Maybe *you* will. I love this house.'

'Sure, honey, so do I. But when the business takes off, we'll be in a whole different league.'

Something was bothering Alice. George was changing and she wasn't sure she liked it. 'You know, ever since you started looking for investors . . .'

George sat up in bed. 'You *wanted* me to expand the business,' he said defensively.

'I just wanted to be happy.'

'You said you didn't mind. You said you would come back to work if we expanded the plant.'

This was a sore point with Alice. She didn't want to return to work. She wanted to stay at home with her children. 'Well . . .'

'It's important,' said George. 'It's important that you come back to work.'

'I know, George, but other things are important too,' she said, trying to make her husband see reason. He had set his priorities; now she wanted to set hers. 'I like being here when the kids get home from school. I don't want someone else taking care of them.'

'We'll find a really good babysitter,' George said. 'Someone responsible. Someone the kids will like.'

'I don't know . . .' Alice said uncertainly. 'It seems like a pretty high price to pay for air fresheners.'

'Air fresheners are my life,' said George.

'My family is mine,' retorted Alice.

They were silent for a moment. George was uneasy, sure that his wife was mad at him.

'Honey . . .' he said.

Suddenly she sat upright in the bed. 'Do you hear something?'

George listened a moment. 'No.'

'I think the TV is on.'

'I'll go check it out,' said George, dragging himself out of bed.

Beethoven had been locked in his dog-run, but he

wasn't quite ready to go to sleep. He burrowed under the fence, using his secret escape route, darted round the Newton home and slipped into the house through an open window in the basement. Beethoven mounted the stairs and wandered into the family room. He snapped on the TV and settled on the sofa to watch the late news.

None of the stories interested him until the newsreader started talking about missing dogs. Beethoven's ears perked right up!

'In the past year,' the man on the news said, 'we've seen a five hundred per cent increase in the reported incidents of stolen pets. Police believe an animal-kidnapping ring is at work.'

What a terrible world we live in, Beethoven thought. Just then, he heard George's footsteps on the stairs. He jumped off the sofa and went into the kitchen.

George came into the family room and stared at the TV. He was sure he had turned it off . . . the kids were in bed, Beethoven was outside. He shrugged and snapped off the television. Maybe he wasn't so sure, after all.

Mr Newton returned to his room and slipped into bed. He noticed that his wife had rolled on her side, pulling the covers up over her head. George was sure she was mad at him.

'You were right. Someone left the TV on.'

Mrs Newton didn't answer. George sniffed his hands. 'You know, no matter how many showers I take, I can always smell Beethoven on me.'

Alice didn't say anything. George was really worried now.

'Are you OK? You're awfully quiet.'

George sighed and rolled over, his back to his wife. 'I guess you're still mad. I guess I don't blame you . . .'

The body next to Mr Newton stirred and rolled. George felt a warm kiss on his ear. He smiled to himself.

'Ooooh. Guess you're not mad at me after all.'

Then he felt a warm lick on his ear, then on his neck. 'So I guess I'm not such a bad guy after all . . .'

The licking got hotter and hotter.

'Wow,' said George, 'this is great!'

Just then, the bathroom door opened and Mrs Newton came out.

'George, who are you talking to?'

Very slowly, George rolled over in the bed, his eyes growing wider and wider. He looked straight into Beethoven's big brown eyes and his drooly mouth. Beethoven gave a long swipe of tongue across Mr Newton's face.

George jumped up as if he had been stung by a bee. 'Ahhhh!' he screamed. 'Out!' He shoved Beethoven out of the bed.

The dog made a dash for the stairs, George Newton right behind him. Man and dog chased each other around the house for a while, then out the back door. George grabbed Beethoven by the collar and tossed him in the dog-run.

'You mangy, disgusting creature!' George paced

angrily back and forth in front of the pen. 'You're never getting out of that pen! Never! Do you hear me? NEVER!'

Beethoven looked genuinely sorry. He put his head on his paws and looked up, as if he were trying to say how sorry he was for being a bad dog. Beethoven wished there were some way he could warn George about what was going to happen next.

'Woof!' said Beethoven.

'Shut up!' screamed Mr Newton.

'Woof!' barked Beethoven.

'I said, be quiet!'

At that very moment, the sprinkler system came on. Suddenly, water gushed up out of the ground, spraying like a shower gone berserk. Cold water blasted up Mr Newton's pyjama leg. There was water on all sides of him and directly under him. In seconds he was drenched.

'YOU LOUSY DOG!' Mr Newton shouted into the spray.

Beethoven watched his master get drenched for a second or two longer. Then he went into his nice dry dog-house and lay down. He yawned and put his head down on his paws. It had been a good day.

CHAPTER ELEVEN

All in all, Beethoven considered himself pretty lucky to have ended up in the Newton home. Sure, George Newton screamed at him from time to time, but Beethoven knew that deep down he didn't *really* mean all the nasty things he said. Yes, Beethoven was blessed with a family he loved, lots of food and a nice little house to live in.

Not quite so lucky was Sparky, who had helped Beethoven escape the dog-nappers all those months ago when he was still a puppy. But Sparky was a pretty tough customer and he had managed to make a life for himself on the streets. He hung out with a homeless man named Clem, who shared his meagre food with the little dog, and they kept each other company. It wasn't as luxurious as Beethoven's life, but it wasn't as bad as it could have been.

Every night, Clem and Sparky went out and rooted around in dustbins, looking for drink cans that Clem took to the recycling centre for five cents apiece.

Clem did most of the work, but Sparky tried to help out. If he found a can, he would do his best to get his jaws around it and carry it back to his master. If he couldn't pick it up, he just rolled it along with his nose.

That night, Sparky and Clem were looking for cans in the town square. Clem was deep in a dustbin and Sparky was trotting back and forth, nose to the ground, looking for the ones that litterbugs had dropped in the gutters.

Sparky saw a can and he went for it, but just as he was about to pounce, the can moved, jerking away a few feet. Sparky cocked his head and stared at the can. He had never seen anything like this before. He ran after the can and it jerked away again!

It had turned into a game now. Sparky was determined to get that can. He chased it around a corner and — bang — a big net came down on him. Vernon and Harvey scooped him up and threw him into a cage in the back of their blue van.

Vernon picked up the can and started winding up the string attached to it. 'See, I told you this would work!'

'Like I said,' agreed Harvey. 'You're a genius.'

They got in the van and drove back to the Dandy Pup Pet Supply warehouse.

When Vernon and Harvey got back, they started unloading the dogs they had captured that night. Sparky was standing up in his cage, growling and showing his teeth. He looked like he was just itching to take a bite out of his captors. He barked angrily. Vernon kicked at the cage.

'Shut up! You'll bother Dr Varnick.'

Up in his office, Dr Varnick was doing his best to see that business remained good. There was a man in his office, a businessman who needed some help from Dandy Pup. He wanted Doc Varnick and his unpleasant concern to do some testing for him.

The businessman had brought two briefcases with him. From one he took out a shiny, heavy gun and two boxes of ammunition.

'I'm in the business of manufacturing guns and bullets,' he said. 'You can imagine how difficult it is to test products like those.'

'You have a real problem,' said Dr Varnick.

'Well, these bullets could be the latest thing in our stock, but there's something we have to know . . .'

'And what might that be?'

'This new type of ammunition we have developed has a special tip. It explodes on contact. We'd like you to use this gun for the tests.'

Dr Varnick weighed the silver revolver in his hand. 'Seems pretty straightforward.'

'We want to know the extent of the damage at close range,' said the businessman.

Dr Varnick nodded. 'I get it. You want to know how messy it is.'

'Exactly. The tests have got to be absolutely accurate,' said the gun manufacturer. 'You can't test these things on little dogs. I presume you can get your hands on the largest breeds in the world? Dogs like Newfoundlands, elkhounds, St Bernards, that kind of thing.'

Doc Varnick frowned. Most of his stock was small dogs, little critters like Sparky that were easy to dog-nap. 'Big dogs are rare, difficult to come by. They're also a lot harder to handle.'

'You turning me down?' asked the businessman.

'Well . . . not exactly. I haven't made up my mind just yet.'

'Maybe I can offer you something that will help you make up your mind.' The man snapped open the latches of the second briefcase and threw back the lid. Inside, the case was packed solid with bundles of hundred-dollar bills.

Doc Varnick took a good, long, hard, loving look at the money and then grinned at the businessman.

'I think we'll be able to take care of you,' he said with an evil grin.

CHAPTER TWELVE

Like most dogs – like most people – Beethoven
didn't like going to the doctor's. But pets – like
people – have to get vaccinations from time to
time, so there was nothing Beethoven could do
about visiting the veterinarian. It fell to Mr Newton
to take him, but Ryce, Ted and Emily went along to
help keep Beethoven's spirits up.

All five of them were sitting in the reception
area, waiting for the vet to see his huge patient,
when an elderly woman came in, an ailing Persian
cat in her arms.

She took the only seat available, one facing
Beethoven and the Newton family. The cat was
mewing pathetically and her owner stroked her,
trying to comfort the big ball of white fur.

'There, there, Pooky,' whispered the lady. 'Soon
we'll see the nice vet-man.'

Pooky, though, wasn't paying any attention to
her mistress. She was looking across the room at
Beethoven, alarmed at being in the same room as a
mountainous dog.

Beethoven was as curious about Pooky as the cat
was about him. Beethoven, being a dog, was not
fond of cats, but he did find them endlessly fascinating.

'Woof!' he said to Pooky. It was more a wary greeting than a threat, but Pooky didn't see it that way. The cat's ears perked up, the fur on her spine stood straight up as if she had been plugged into an electric socket, and she screeched in alarm. Then she went limp in her owner's arms.

'Pooky!' screamed the lady.

'Beethoven!' yelled Mr Newton.

'Pooky! Pooky!' the lady looked bewildered. 'My cat! She's fainted!'

'I didn't know cats *could* faint,' whispered Ted.

'Neither did I,' said Ryce.

Mr Newton and Pooky's owner were busy trying to revive the cat. It took a few moments, but gradually the groggy cat came around. She looked a little dazed and dizzy.

'I think we'll wait outside,' said Pooky's owner.

'That might be better,' agreed Mr Newton. He glowered at Beethoven. 'Behave!' he ordered.

Beethoven dipped his head in shame and drooled a little on the linoleum floor.

They had to wait a long time for the vet, so Emily occupied herself with sucking her thumb.

George Newton shook his head in disgust. 'How can you put your thumb in your mouth after touching these chairs?'

'It's a sign of immaturity,' announced Ryce.

'Immature?' said Emily. 'I'm only five years old.'

'Well,' chimed in Ted, 'the dentist says it wrecks your teeth.'

71

Emily didn't even bother to take her thumb out of her mouth. She spoke around it. 'You should talk, Ted. You scratch your butt when you sleep.'

'So what?' Ted retorted. 'It keeps me from sucking my thumb, doesn't it?'

Emily looked unconvinced.

'Do you know how dirty these chairs are?' asked her father. 'Animals sit on them and lean on them, and when animals get nervous, they shed, they perspire, they go to the bathroom.'

That was all the convincing Emily needed. Her thumb came out of her mouth so fast it popped.

Just then, the vet's nurse came into the room. 'The doctor will see you now.'

Beethoven took his place on the stainless-steel examining-table and looked around him nervously. He could detect the smells of hundreds of animals in the room and he wasn't sure that he liked the position he found himself in. His ears kept on perking up. Somewhere beyond the examination room were cages where sick animals were kept for treatment, and from time to time the dogs barked or whined to be released.

To Beethoven, the vet's office was a pretty creepy place.

Emily, Ted and Ryce didn't care much for it either.

'Daddy,' asked Emily in a very small, very worried voice. 'Is the vet going to hurt Beethoven?'

Mr Newton was quick to reassure his daughter. 'Honey, nothing can hurt Beethoven.'

Beethoven gave Mr Newton a look as if to say: Don't be so sure about it.

'Dad,' whispered Ted, 'is he going to have to have any s-h-o-t-s?'

'You don't have to spell it out, Ted,' explained Mr Newton. 'Beethoven's a dog. He doesn't understand English and he certainly can't spell. But in answer to your question, yes.'

At the mention of s-h-o-t-s, Beethoven's ears shot straight up like pieces of toast coming out of a toaster. He threw back his head and howled as loud as he could.

The instant he started to howl, the other creatures in the holding-cages began to howl. Suddenly, the whole animal clinic seemed to be alive with the anguished howls of dozens of dogs.

In the middle of the din, the vet came into the room and said hello – and it was Dr Varnick, the evil owner of Dandy Pup Pet Supply! Gradually, the howling died down, but Beethoven kept his eyes on the doctor. There was something about this man he didn't like at all.

'I'm sorry about all the noise,' said Mr Newton.

'That's OK. It's all part of being a vet.' He patted Beethoven on the head, appraising him. 'This is Beethoven? Magnificent animal.' Dr Varnick was thinking that an animal of Beethoven's size would be perfect for the ammunition test.

The doctor turned to get something from the medicine cabinet. When he turned around, he was holding a giant hypodermic needle in his hands. Beethoven's eyes grew wide as he took in the size of the needle, then his eyelids fluttered and closed. He swayed for a moment, then toppled like a skyscraper in an earthquake.

All of the Newtons and Dr Varnick stared at Beethoven, who lay sprawled on the floor.

'He fainted,' said Dr Varnick.

'I didn't know dogs could faint too,' said Ted.

It wasn't such a bad thing that Beethoven fainted when he did, because when he was out like a light like that, he was much easier to deal with. The vet gave him his injections and woke him up and told the Newtons that Beethoven could leave. Beethoven needed no further encouragement. He scrambled to his feet and headed for the door, Mr Newton trying to drag him back with the leash.

'He might be a little groggy this evening,' said Dr Varnick.

Mr Newton was fighting with Beethoven like a deep-sea fisherman struggling to land a marlin. 'That would be nice.'

Dr Varnick took a deep breath. 'Mr Newton,' he said quietly, 'I wonder if I could have a word with you in private?'

'Sure,' said Mr Newton. He passed the leash to Ryce, who was immediately yanked towards the door. 'Take Beethoven to the car. I'll be right there.'

'OK, Dad,' Ryce called over her shoulder as Beethoven hauled her out into the car-park.

'Come into my office a moment, please,' said Dr Varnick. He looked very grave.

Suddenly, Mr Newton was worried. 'Is there a problem? Is Beethoven sick?' Maybe the doctor had noticed something during the routine visit.

Dr Varnick settled himself behind his grey metal desk, George Newton facing him.

'I feel I have a duty to inform you that St Bernards have been quite heavily bred. Overbred, really.'

'What does that have to do with Beethoven?' Mr Newton asked, still puzzled and a little worried.

'Nothing specifically. I've been reading a lot recently about St Bernards in the veterinary journals – there's been quite a bit written about certain behavioural problems with the breed.'

'Problems with the breed? I don't get it.'

'More and more, overbred St Bernards have been known to turn on people. They can attack without provocation. I only mention it because you have children.'

'Wait ... You're trying to tell me that *Beethoven* might attack one of my kids?'

'It's a possibility,' said Dr Varnick.

'Are you sure?'

'No one can be absolutely sure about the animal mind, Mr Newton.'

George Newton nodded. That was doubly true of an animal mind like Beethoven's!

The instant Mr Newton got home, he told his wife what the vet had said. Mrs Newton couldn't believe her ears.

'That's crazy,' she insisted. 'There isn't anything remotely dangerous about Beethoven.'

They were sitting on the patio of their house. Out on the lawn, Emily and Beethoven were playing, rolling and running on the grass. The little girl's delighted giggles floated up to where the two adults sat.

'Maybe not,' agreed Mr Newton. 'Not so far, but who knows?'

Alice Newton smiled. 'He might take a piece out of you, dear, but I know he would never hurt the kids. Not in a million years.' She watched the dog playing with her little daughter and smiled, 'Yeah, he's a real killer, that Beethoven.'

To Mr Newton it was not a laughing matter. 'I know you think I might use this as an excuse to get rid of him. I wouldn't.'

'I know you wouldn't,' said Mrs Newton quietly.

'But I have to warn you — at the first sign of anything out of the ordinary, he goes.'

'George . . .'

'No, you have to be firm about things like this. A snarl, a snap, a funny look, and he's gone.' Mr Newton sounded very resolute. 'And that has nothing to do with his history with me.'

CHAPTER THIRTEEN

Much as she didn't want to, Alice eventually gave in and agreed to work at Newton Air Fresheners. George convinced her that he really needed the extra help and that he couldn't yet afford to hire someone else and pay an extra salary. Alice made her husband promise that as soon as she was able to, she could go back to being a housewife. In the meantime, Mrs Newton had to find someone to look after her kids in the afternoon.

Devonia Peet was a neighbour of the Newtons. She said she would take care of Emily, Ryce and Ted after school — Devonia needed a little extra money.

Alice and all three of her children felt a little glum as they trudged up the street to Devonia's house for the first time, but Mrs Newton did her best to keep spirits up.

'You guys are really going to have a great time at Devonia's,' she said with all the enthusiasm she could muster.

'I don't need a babysitter,' said Ryce sourly.

'Actually, Mom,' chimed in Ted, 'there's really no stigma attached to being a latchkey kid these days.'

'Why can't Beethoven take care of us?' asked Emily.

'Beethoven has to stay in the garden, honey.'

'Why?'

Alice stopped and sighed sadly. 'Aw, c'mon, guys! It isn't going to do us any good to go into this with a bad attitude. OK?'

'Mom?' asked Emily in a very small voice. 'How come you have to go back to work, anyway?'

Alice was on the verge of saying something, but there was no point in making her children resent their father. Instead, she tried to make her voice bright. 'You guys are just going to love Devonia.'

Devonia was on the front steps of her house, waiting to greet them. She was a large woman with too much make-up and dyed red hair. She wore a brown dress with great big splotches of pink on it.

'Hi, y'all! How y'all doin'?' She leaned down close to Emily. 'Ya little cutie!' She pinched Emily's plump cheek.

'Ow,' Emily said.

'Don't worry about a thing, Mrs Newton. We're going to get along great. Right, kids?'

Ryce rolled her eyes. 'Yeah, right,' she said sarcastically.

Quickly, Alice Newton kissed her children goodbye, trying not to see the pleading look in their eyes, silently begging her not to leave them.

'Now you be good,' she whispered. 'Be brave. And I'll be back at six.'

Devonia hustled the kids into her house. 'OK. We're gonna do all kinds of neat stuff. I was hopin' we could sing a little tune together. You guys like music?'

'What kind of music?' asked Ryce suspiciously.

'Well . . . how 'bout Herb Alpert and the Tijuana Brass? Or maybe you like some of the newer sounds. I'm a nut for the disco beat.' Devonia grinned. She had lipstick on her teeth. 'It puts the bump in my rump, ya know? Don't know why it went out of fashion.'

'That *is* a mystery,' said Ryce disdainfully.

Mrs Newton was not in a very good mood by the time she got to Newton Air Fresheners — she was certainly in no mood to put up with the oh-so-hip Brie and Brad, but she gritted her teeth and did so, for the sake of her husband.

Brad and Brie were in George's office when Mrs Newton got there.

'So,' said Brad, 'you're re-entering the workforce, huh, Alice?'

Alice smiled tightly. 'I guess I am.'

'Good for you,' said Brie. 'You are too much on the ball to just be a housewife.'

Alice was about to say something equally nasty back, but George Newton shot his wife a warning look.

'So,' he said quickly, 'I guess you've had some time to think about —'

'Yes,' said Brie decisively, 'we've made our decision.'

George tensed.

'Yes,' said Brad. He smiled broadly. 'We have decided we want to get into bed with Newton Air Fresheners!'

George jumped to his feet. 'We have a deal? That's fantastic! That's just fantastic, isn't it, Alice?'

'Fantastic,' said Alice cautiously. She still didn't like Brad and Brie.

'We want to get this deal going as quickly as possible,' said Brie.

'We're meeting with our lawyer today. We could go over the paperwork tonight,' said Brad.

'Let us take you to dinner,' said Brie. 'Are there any good restaurants in this area?'

George and Alice exchanged glances quickly. George seemed to be appealing for help.

Mrs Newton smiled. 'Why don't you come for a barbecue at our house?'

'Your house?' said Brie. She looked sort of doubtful, as if Mrs Newton might not know how to cook.

'It would be more relaxing,' said Alice brightly. 'You can talk.'

Brie looked to Brad. 'What do you think?'

'I like it,' said Brad with a big toothy grin. 'Regional American cuisine is in. Very hot! It would be educational.'

'Why not!' said Brie. 'Let's live dangerously!'

Devonia was true to her word. She loved disco! She sat at an organ playing 'Lady Marmalade' at top-volume and singing her lungs out. Ryce and Ted sat in the background, trying to do their homework. Emily had got bored and had wandered outside. She was on the lawn, playing with a ball.

Devonia stopped singing for a moment. 'Hey, let's have a little help with this swingin' song!'

Ryce and Ted didn't look up from their homework, but they sang along to be polite.

'Hey sister, go sister, soul sister, go sister!' sang Ted.

'Hey sister, go sister, soul sister, go sister!' sang Ryce.

No one was paying any attention to Emily. Her ball had fallen into the swimming-pool and she was leaning over the edge, trying to reach it. She stretched a little too far and toppled into the water! She sank down and then bobbed to the surface.

'Help! Somebody!' she screamed. Emily thrashed in the water, trying to keep herself afloat. 'Help!'

But Ted, Ryce and Devonia couldn't hear her frantic cries for help over the loud organ music and the singing.

Sitting in his dog-pen down the street, Beethoven's ears popped up. *He* heard Emily! He jumped to his feet and whimpered, pawing at the gate. Mr Newton had filled in his escape route!

'Help!' called Emily.

Devonia was singing as loud as she possibly could. 'Gitchee, gitchee, ya-ya, da-da. Gitchee, gitchee, ya-ya, hee-ya. Mocha, chocolata, ya-ya . . .'

Beethoven was growing frantic. He threw all of his weight against the gate, snapping the lock. Then he was off and running towards the sound of Emily's voice.

Devonia stopped singing, but kept on pounding

out a tune on the keyboard. 'You kids might be interested to know that I'm the feature performer Saturday nights at the Padded Zebra,' she yelled over the racket of her own playing. 'You and your folks might like to stop in. They have the world's most fattening salad bar.'

Beethoven raced up the street and charged into Devonia's backyard. Without hesitation, he dived into the pool. All one hundred and eighty-five pounds of thundering dog hit the surface like a cannon-ball, sending up a huge, drenching wave of water. He plunged down deep and grabbed Emily and tossed her on to his back. Emily surfaced like a submarine and Beethoven dragged her to the shallow end and out of the pool to safety.

Emily coughed and sputtered and rubbed her eyes. Beethoven sat next to her, licking her face and looking very concerned.

Music was still blasting out of the house.

Emily hugged the sopping wet dog. 'Thank you, Beethoven. You saved my life!'

Beethoven licked her again. It was nothing, he wanted to say.

'But you better go home now. Mom said you had to stay in the backyard. It was an order.' Very gently, she pushed Beethoven away. He whimpered, licked her again and walked away sadly.

Ryce was bored with Devonia's blabbing and dreadful singing. She looked up from her homework to gaze out of the window.

'Hey! What's going on? Emily fell in the pool!' Emily was standing at the window, sopping wet.

Devonia stopped playing and jumped to her feet. 'The pool! Why, that little . . .'

All three of them ran outside. Devonia was scared and angry. 'Who said you could go in the pool, young lady!' She grabbed Emily roughly and shook her by the shoulders. 'What are you trying to do? Get me in trouble?'

Emily started to cry. She was scared and cold and wet and she wanted to go home. 'Mommy!' she cried.

'Hey,' shouted Ryce angrily. 'Leave my sister alone!'

'Emily,' hollered Ted, 'are you all right?'

Emily did her best to stop crying. She was glad that her brother and sister were sticking up for her. 'I'm OK.'

'What were you doing in the pool?' demanded Devonia.

'I fell in.'

Ryce hugged Emily. 'Oh, Emily! You must have been so scared!'

Emily nodded. 'I thought I was going to die.'

It was Devonia's turn to be scared. She realized that she should not have been playing the organ and entertaining herself. She *should* have been watching the children. Devonia composed herself and tried to act as nice and as sweet as pie.

'Aw, you poor little thing. You were never in any real danger now, were you?' She tried to give her a hug, but Emily pulled away.

'We don't want you to get into trouble,' Devonia said with a wink, 'so we'll just let this be our little secret.'

'I'd like to call my mother, please,' said Ryce coldly.

Devonia gulped. 'Your mother?'

'Immediately!'

Alice dashed out of the Newton factory fast — she didn't care what George thought. She was at Devonia's house in five minutes flat. She loaded her children in the car, doing her best not to lose her temper.

Devonia prattled nervously. 'She must have sneaked out while I was watching Ted and Ryce. It was hot out, so I guess she wanted to take a little swim.'

'And where were you?' asked Alice. She got into the car and slammed the door.

Devonia leaned in the window. 'Where was I? I was where I was supposed to be. Inside. Watching the other two. If Emily had stayed where I put her, none of this would have happened. If you ask me, what these children need is discipline.'

Alice looked furious. 'What these children need is their mother.' She slammed the car into gear. 'You're fired!'

CHAPTER FOURTEEN

Things were pretty tense in the Newton house that night. There had been the bad scare with Emily in Devonia's pool, and then Mrs Newton had to go home and prepare dinner for Brie and Brad. She was furious that because she had to go and work with her husband, her youngest child had been put in great danger. She was ready to resign immediately, and never mind how that affected the business!

Mrs Newton was in the kitchen, trying to keep calm while she prepared dinner. Mr Newton left his guests on the patio to come in to reason with her.

'Honey,' he said softly, 'we can't throw out the option of a babysitter just because we got a bad one.'

'Emily could have drowned!' said Mrs Newton angrily.

'We'll find someone better to look after the kids.'

'Over my dead body!' Alice whirled around, a frying-pan in her hand. Mr Newton winced, as if she were about to belt him with it. But she managed to control herself. 'Where are the kids?' she asked.

'They're outside charming our guests,' said George. 'See, honey, we're all doing our best here . . .'

To be honest, Ted, Ryce and Emily were not

being all that charming. They sat across from Brad and Brie, staring at them coldly. The Newton kids didn't know anything about the air-freshener business or investments — all they knew was that because of Brie and Brad, they had to go to a babysitter every afternoon when school was out.

Mr Newton had tethered Beethoven far away, out on the lawn. Not close enough to bother the guests.

Brad and Brie felt a little uncomfortable around children, particularly children who seemed to dislike them as much as the Newton kids did.

'So,' asked Brad, 'don't you kids have any homework or something?'

'No,' said Emily.

Brad and Brie exchanged a look. They really wished these children would go away.

'You know,' said Brad, 'we're fine on our own. You don't have to entertain us.'

'Go out and play,' suggested Brie.

'We *are* out,' said Ted.

This irritated Brie. 'Then go *in* and play.'

'We're supposed to keep you company,' explained Ryce. 'At least, we're supposed to stay here until Mom and Dad finish their fight.'

'It's not necessary,' said Brad, flashing a phoney smile. 'Really.'

The kids exchanged looks. They desperately wanted to get out of there.

'OK,' they said.

'If you're sure,' added Ryce.

'We're sure,' said Brie firmly.

Ted paused a moment. 'Can I ask you something?'

'Sure,' said Brad.

'Do you have kids?'

Before Brad and Brie could answer, Emily blurted out, 'What do you think?'

Ted shrugged. 'No, I guess not.'

Brad and Brie waited until the kids went inside, then reached down and pulled some paperwork out of a briefcase. With the children out of the picture, Brad thought he and Brie were alone. He forgot about Beethoven. He was still tethered on the lawn, but he was watching every move and listening to every word.

Brad smiled at his partner. 'If we pull this off tonight, in six months we'll *own* Newton Air Fresheners.'

'All we have to do is get George to sign these papers without him reading them too closely,' Brie said.

'No problem,' said Brad with a laugh. 'George will do exactly what we tell him to do.'

Alice and George were still furious with each other, but they had guests and they knew they had to do their best to make them feel at home. They came out on to the patio and Alice got busy setting the table. George put a tray of snacks down in front of Brad and Brie. He grinned, looking slightly embarrassed.

'Sorry for the delay,' he said. 'We just had a tiny family crisis to iron out.'

'No problem,' said Brie with a wave of her hand.

Brad was more businesslike. He slid his papers under George's nose. 'Here's the contract. Take a quick look.' He uncapped his fancy fountain pen and put it in Mr Newton's hand. 'You sign on the bottom line.'

George Newton looked through the pages. There was lots of dense type and he shook his head as he looked at it. 'I'll have to take a close look at –'

Brie leaned forward. 'George, do tell me about your beautiful dog.'

Mr Newton looked up, puzzled. Why would Brie want to talk about Beethoven at a time like this? 'Our dog?'

Brad could see what Brie was doing. She was trying to distract George, trying to prevent him reading the contract too closely. 'He's a pure-bred St Bernard, isn't he?'

'We think so,' said George uncertainly. His eyes dropped down to the contract again.

Brie stood up. 'I just *love* big dumb-looking animals,' she said, clapping her hands together. 'I want a closer look at this big lug!' She walked over to Beethoven and unhooked his leash from its mooring and walked him back to the patio. 'Dogs are so much easier to get along with than children!' she exclaimed.

Brie slipped the leash under the table leg and then leaned down, thrusting her face into Beethoven's. 'Hello, cutsie-wootsie doggie-woo.' Beethoven looked faintly sick. 'Mama loves great big doggie-woggies!' His expression changed. Now it looked as if he wouldn't have minded taking a bite out of her sleek leg.

Brad was very anxious to get Mr Newton to sign the contract.

'The place you're supposed to sign is marked in yellow,' he said.

Alice didn't think they should rush into anything, and she saw that Brad and Brie were pressurizing her husband into signing. It was very unlike George not to go through legal documents very carefully, but she could see that his natural caution was being worn down.

'Hold on now, George,' she protested. 'Why do we have to sign these things right now?'

Brie acted fast. She knocked over her water glass to create a diversion. 'I'm so sorry.'

Alice immediately started mopping up. 'No problem. Don't get up. I'll take care of it.' She ran into the house to get a sponge, and Brad and Brie closed in on George.

'It's a straightforward agreement, George,' said Brad. 'Standard for all our investments.'

'Yeah, but . . .'

Beethoven was on his feet now, wandering around the table and weaving in and out of Brie and Brad's chair legs, circling them with his leash.

'We really have to get going here, George,' said Brie urgently. 'Of course, if you don't *want* our money –'

George really wanted the money. 'OK,' he said.

'I guess everything is in order.' Just as he put the pen to the paper, Beethoven pushed his big head under George's hand, as if demanding attention. Beethoven's tongue slithered between Mr Newton's fingers.

'Hey there! Stop it, Beethoven.' He shoved his dog away and Beethoven nervously slipped under the table, further tangling the leash in Brad and Brie's chair legs.

Alice came out of the kitchen and quickly wiped up the spilt water. 'Did I miss anything?' she asked, nervously eyeing the contract.

'George has looked everything over, right, George?'

'It's all standard stuff,' agreed George. Once again he put Brad's pen to the paper and once again Beethoven pushed his head up from under the table, nudging his hand.

Brad was angry now. 'Darn dog!' He snatched up Beethoven's red ball and threw it as far and as hard as he could. 'Go fetch!'

OK, thought Beethoven. He took off, streaking after the ball like an arrow. About four or five feet of the leash played out before it took hold of the table and Brad and Brie's chairs. Suddenly, they were yanked under the table, tipping it over and smashing everything on it.

George and Alice jumped to their feet in horror, but Brad and Brie were tangled in their chairs. As Beethoven charged across the lawn, Brad and Brie were pulled after him, rocketing along behind the big dog, the table in tow. Both of them were screaming at the tops of their lungs!

The ball had landed in the neighbour's garden and Beethoven flew over the low fence like a hairy 747, still pulling Brad and Brie behind him. They hit the fence feet first, the impact sending them head over heels over the fence. They landed upright on the ground, still tied to their chairs, and a second later the table fell out of the sky and dropped right in front of them.

Brad and Brie were too dazed, too stunned, to speak. They were covered with dirt and grass, their perfect clothes reduced to rags.

Beethoven picked up the ball, dropped it at Brad's feet and smiled.

George Newton was angrier than he had ever been in his whole life. He charged across the lawn, murder in his eyes. 'BEETHOVEN!' he screamed.

Beethoven took one look at his enraged master and decided to get out of there. He shot off across the neighbour's lawn. Brad and Brie bolted forward, their chairs ploughing a furrow in the lawn.

Beethoven was running hard, his tongue blowing in the wind. He looked over his shoulder and saw Brie and Brad holding on for dear life. He hoped they were having as much fun as he was!

CHAPTER FIFTEEN

Hours after Brad and Brie had picked themselves up and limped away, George Newton was still in shock. There was now no chance that Brad and Brie would put money into Newton Air Fresheners. He sat in a chair on the patio, staring for minutes at a time at the deep grooves in the lawn. Alice sat with him, afraid he would fall apart. The kids were in the house, standing just inside the patio door, listening to their parents. Beethoven was keeping his distance, hanging out in his dog-house at the far end of the yard.

'The people who were ready to bankroll our expansion and solve our financial problems,' said George sadly, 'ploughed our yard with their butts.'

'I didn't like those people,' said Alice. 'I don't trust them and I don't want their money.'

'But the business,' said George weakly.

'I don't suppose my opinion matters, but I really don't care about expanding the business. If I had been home today, Emily would not have fallen in that pool. I'm not re-entering the workforce. You'll expand the business somehow, George. You'll make your fortune and tucked away, deep in the shadows, will be me and the kids.'

George Newton looked at his wife. He was

shocked and deeply offended. 'Suddenly I'm a lousy father and husband. Is that how you see me? That's nice. Everything was fine until we brought that dog into our lives.'

'Beethoven has nothing to do with it,' protested Alice.

'Oh yeah? Who did that?' He pointed at the twin trenches in the lawn. 'I've been patient. I've tried. And I've had it! The dog has *got* to go!'

On the other side of the patio door, Ryce, Ted and Emily exchanged worried looks. This time it sounded like their father really meant what he said.

Alice knew it was time to stand up to her husband. Her voice was quiet and calm, but defiant. 'I'm proud of Beethoven. Those two morons insulted your kids and dangled their money in your face until you grovelled. Beethoven was the only one of us who had the nerve to give those jerks the ride they deserved.' She stood up. 'That's all I have to say. I'm going to bed.'

George shook his head slowly. 'My dream's going down the drain and you're worried about a dog.'

'Your family is going down the drain,' Alice shot back, 'and you're worried about a dream.'

George was left alone in the yard with his thoughts. Beethoven looked at him quizzically for a moment, then turned his back on him and fell asleep.

The next day was Saturday, and Ted, Ryce and

Emily had a plan. They got up very early, deter-mined to give their father a totally hassle-free morn-ing. The idea was that they would make everything so perfect that he would be in a good mood and they would be able to talk him into allowing Beethoven to remain a part of the family.

Emily was in charge of feeding Beethoven, which she did, but not before she accidentally emptied a fifty-pound bag of dry dog food all over the kitchen floor. Ryce and Ted had to clean it up. Ted walked Beethoven, who dragged him all the way down the street and all the way back again. The three kids helped wash Beethoven and he repaid the favour by shaking off the excess water and soaking them all.

By the time Mr Newton came down that morn-ing, a perfect breakfast was waiting for him on the kitchen table. Ryce, Ted and Emily were standing next to the table like waiters in a high-class restaur-ant.

'What's this?' asked Mr Newton.

'We made you breakfast, Dad,' said Ted.

Ryce pulled out her father's chair. 'Scrambled eggs, just the way you like them.'

George nodded and sat down. 'I have a feeling I know what this is all about.'

'I fed Beethoven,' said Emily proudly.

'And we washed him,' added Ryce. 'He smells great!'

'You should smell him, Daddy,' said Emily.

'I'm going to walk him every day,' said Ted.

'We divided up the dog chores,' explained Ryce.

'You won't have anything to do with Beethoven from now on.'

Mr Newton picked up his fork. 'I see.'

'Is there anything else I can get you, Dad?' asked Ted.

'No,' said Mr Newton, 'I'm fine. Thank you.' He dug into his scrambled eggs and immediately felt something go crunch between his teeth.

'I dropped part of an eggshell in there, Dad,' said Emily. 'If I were you, I'd chew carefully.'

'So what do you think?' asked Ryce. 'Do we get to keep Beethoven?'

George, chewing carefully, thought for a moment. 'Well, I think –'

Just then the doorbell rang and the children didn't get a chance to find out exactly what their father thought.

CHAPTER SIXTEEN

Alice opened the door to Dr Varnick. He was smiling nervously and his eyes seemed buggier than usual behind the thick lenses of his glasses.

'Sorry to bother you, Mrs Newton. I'm Dr Varnick, your vet.'

'Is there something wrong? Is there some problem with Beethoven?'

'No, not that I know of. I was passing by and I thought I would look in on him. With an animal as large as yours, I like to do a follow-up on rabies shots. See how he's doing.'

Mrs Newton led the vet through the house and out to the dog-run in the backyard. 'That's awfully kind of you, Dr Varnick.'

Beethoven looked at the vet rather suspiciously as Alice unlocked the gate to the dog-run. 'There you go,' she said.

'I won't be a moment,' said Varnick.

'I'll be in the house if you need me,' said Mrs Newton.

Dr Varnick looked over his shoulder, then slipped into the run and knelt down next to Beethoven. He didn't notice Emily watching him from the upstairs window of her room. 'How you doing, boy?' He reached into the pocket of his jacket and pulled out a pair of surgical scissors. Quickly, he cut into his sleeve and tore the cloth back as far as the elbow. He squirted fake blood from a hidden tube on to his forearm, and then smeared some of the red goo on to Beethoven's mouth and snout.

Beethoven was scared and puzzled by what the doctor was doing, and he was totally unprepared for what happened next. Suddenly, the vet reared back and hit Beethoven as hard as he could on the side of the head!

Beethoven had never been hit before and he pulled back in shock and terror. Dr Varnick was angry. He couldn't get Beethoven to react to his harsh treatment.

'Come on,' grumbled the vet. 'Come on, you big stupid mutt!' He smacked Beethoven hard on the nose. That hurt! Beethoven snapped at the vet and barked ferociously.

'That's it,' growled Varnick. He grabbed Beethoven's collar and yanked him over on top of him. Then he shouted at the top of his lungs. 'Help! Help!'

Beethoven barked and howled and tried to get free, but Varnick held him tightly.

The whole Newton family was out on the lawn in a matter of seconds. George and Alice immediately threw themselves on Beethoven and pulled him off the vet. Alice looked at Dr Varnick in horror. 'Oh no! Beethoven bit you!'

Varnick cradled his bloody arm and stumbled to his feet.

'What happened?' demanded George.

'He just lunged at me and —'

'That's not true!' yelled Emily. 'I saw the whole thing!'

'Saw the whole thing?' said Mr Newton. 'How?'

She pointed to her bedroom window. 'I was watching from my room. I saw you! I saw you hit Beethoven!'

'Emily!' said Alice. 'Stop it!'

Dr Varnick did his best to control his voice. 'Why would I hit Beethoven? I patted him on the head. Maybe from a distance the little girl —'

'Liar!' shouted Emily.

'Emily,' ordered Mr Newton. 'Be quiet!'

'No, please,' said Varnick. 'It's perfectly natural for a child to defend her dog.'

'I'm going to call an ambulance,' said George.

An ambulance was the *last* thing Dr Varnick wanted. 'No. It's all right, Mr Newton. I'll take care of it.'

'Please,' pleaded George. 'Come into the house and let us help you.'

But Dr Varnick would accept no more help than a teatowel that he wrapped around his arm.

'I'm so sorry,' said George Newton. 'He's never done anything like this before.'

Dr Varnick walked to his car. 'Once an animal has crossed the line and attacked a human, you can be assured he'll do it again. And it may well be one of your children.'

'I can't believe it.'

Dr Varnick got behind the wheel of his car. 'There are laws about this kind of thing,' he said stiffly. 'If you don't bring the animal to my office immediately, I'll have to go to the authorities and press charges.'

Mr Newton walked slowly back to his family, who were waiting nervously in the back garden. This time it really did seem like the end for Beethoven.

CHAPTER SEVENTEEN

The day that had begun with such promise ended with sadness. Alice Newton spent hours trying to comfort her children, but each one of them refused to be reassured.

'It's going to be all right,' she said over and over again.

'Mom,' said Ryce, 'you have to listen to Emily!'

'Emily may not understand what she saw, honey.'

Emily started to cry. 'Dad doesn't believe me because he hates Beethoven! He always hated Beethoven!'

'I'll talk to Daddy,' said Alice. But she already knew that it would do no good.

Mr Newton didn't want to get rid of Beethoven, but the law was the law, and his family wasn't making things easy for him.

'What are we going to do?' Mrs Newton asked. 'Do we have to have Beethoven' — she could hardly bring herself to say it — 'destroyed?'

George sighed heavily. 'Yes.'

'But we can't. He's part of the family.'

'I know,' said Mr Newton wearily. 'But we have no choice. It's the law.'

'George.'

'I'd better get it over with,' he said.

Beethoven stood up and wagged his tail hopefully when Mr Newton approached, carrying the leash. Maybe he was just going to take him for a walk.

When George looked at Beethoven's loving brown eyes, he felt himself go weak, his determination wavering. But he steeled himself. He *had* to do it.

'Come on, boy,' he said softly. He clipped the leash to Beethoven's collar and led him out of the run to the station wagon. Just as he was pulling out of the driveway, the front door of the house flew open and Ryce, Ted and Emily came running out.

'Daddy, no!'

'Beethoven!'

'Don't go! Please come back!'

Mr Newton could only try to shut his ears against their misery. He drove away, with Beethoven looking sadly out of the back window of the car at the children he loved and who he might never see again.

It was the worst ride of George Newton's life. He kept looking in the rear-view mirror at Beethoven watching him with miserable eyes.

'This isn't personal,' said Mr Newton softly. 'My father once had to do this. He drove our dog to the vet to have him put down. I hated him for doing it and now I'm doing it myself.' It was hard being a grown up, he thought.

'I know you don't believe me. And the kids will never believe me. But I don't want to do this.' There was a catch in his voice and, for a moment,

Mr Newton was afraid he would break down and cry. He cleared his throat. 'You love the kids, Beethoven, so I *know* you understand that this has to be done.'

Beethoven looked at George's eyes in the mirror, dejected but dignified.

Dr Varnick was waiting when Mr Newton and Beethoven got to the animal hospital.

'You're doing the right thing, Mr Newton,' said the vet. 'It's hard, I know, but you have to do it.'

George nodded glumly. 'I suppose. How's the arm?'

Dr Varnick had wrapped his arm in a phoney bandage. 'Thirty-seven stitches,' he said with a grimace.

'I'm so sorry.'

'These things happen to a vet, Mr Newton.' Dr Varnick led Beethoven into the kennel room at the back of the clinic. 'Do you want to keep his collar and tags? Some people do,' said the doctor.

'I guess so.' George knelt down and unhooked Beethoven's collar and leash. Beethoven licked Mr Newton's face tenderly, as if to say: I know what's happening here and I know it's not your fault. I forgive you for everything.

George wiped his cheek and stared deep into Beethoven's eyes. Then he touched him lovingly on the neck. Then he gave him a hug. At that moment, for the first time, they seemed truly to love one another. It felt, finally, as if they belonged together – and it was too late.

Dr Varnick could see that Mr Newton was beginning to weaken. The vet had gone to a lot of trouble to get this dog and he wasn't about to let him slip away now. 'It's a very sad state of affairs, Mr Newton. But it's got to be done.' He slipped a choke-collar over Beethoven's head. 'Come on, boy,' he said, leading him into the cage, as if putting him in a prison cell.

A huge lump rose in Mr Newton's throat and he brushed away a tear. 'Bye, Beethoven,' he said huskily. 'I'm sorry.'

Dr Varnick's receptionist stopped George on the way out. 'We'll have to charge for a day's boarding,' she said briskly. 'The man who does our lethal injections and disposals doesn't work today. So we'll have to hold the dog overnight. Shall we bill you?'

George hardly heard her. 'That would be fine,' he said as he plodded towards the door.

When George Newton got home, his children wouldn't look at him, wouldn't talk to him, wouldn't even be in the same room with him. They filed out of the kitchen as soon as he entered.

'Kids, please, I –'

Emily was the only one who would speak to him. 'Dog killer,' she said.

As George was going out of the front door of the hospital, Beethoven was being led out of the back. Vernon and Harvey had him muzzled and were dragging him towards the van. Dr Varnick watched them, his shirt-sleeves rolled up. He had taken off the phoney bandage and was very pleased indeed, thinking of those hundred-dollar bills.

'Sure is a nice specimen, Doc,' said Vernon. 'Perfect for the ammo experiment.'

'Yeah!' Dr Varnick smiled. 'He'll probably take a couple of bullets.'

Harvey was inside the van, trying to drag in Beethoven, but the dog dug in his heels and refused to budge.

'Stubborn son of a gun,' Harvey grumbled.

'I'll handle it,' said Vernon. He pulled a short piece of rubber hose from his belt and wacked Beethoven hard on the haunches. Beethoven yelped and jumped into the van.

'I'll be by soon,' Varnick said to his evil henchmen. 'Have everything ready. We'll run the experiment on him first thing in the morning.'

'We hear you, Doc,' said Vernon. He started the van and drove out of the car-park.

CHAPTER EIGHTEEN

Harvey and Vernon were having trouble getting Beethoven out of the van and into a cage in the Dandy Pup Pet Supply warehouse. Beethoven was growling and baring his fangs. He could smell the other dogs in the giant room and their scent told him that he was in danger.

Vernon decided that Beethoven could not be moved by hand. 'Harvey, get the pole,' he ordered.

'The pole?'

'Is there an echo in here?' yelled Vernon. 'I want the pole! Now get it!'

'Do you have to yell at me? This is what really bothers me. I'm right next to you. I can hear you perfectly. Talk to me in a normal tone of voice.'

Vernon grabbed Harvey by the neck, choking him. Harvey's eyes bulged out of their sockets. 'Harvey,' said Vernon in a normal tone, 'could you please get the pole now? I'd really appreciate it.'

Harvey nodded frantically, his eyes popping. Vernon let go of his assistant and Harvey dropped to the floor, gagging and coughing.

'Was that better, Harvey?'

'Yeah,' said Harvey hoarsely. He got the pole. It was a long aluminium rod with a leather handle on one end and a wide wire loop on the other. Vernon looped the coil around Beethoven's neck and pulled it tight, like a noose. He dragged poor Beethoven out of the van and hauled him into the kennel room.

The instant Harvey and Vernon got him in there, all the dogs in their dirty, rusty cages started to bark and howl. Beethoven barked back. His old pal Sparky jumped to his feet and barked.

Beethoven was amazed to see the feisty little dog and he woofed at him wildly. He was saying: You helped me escape once when I was a pup. Now it's my turn!

'Enough chit-chat!' shouted Vernon. He and Harvey shoved Beethoven into his cage. Beethoven looked at them with hate in his eyes. He growled and snarled.

Vernon laughed at him. 'The Doc will work on you first thing in the morning, big guy. Then you'll be one dead puppy.'

The Newton house was covered in gloom. George sat glumly on the patio, watching his wife gather up the dog toys surrounding Beethoven's old house.

Mr Newton's face was a mask of anguish. 'Tell me,' he said quietly. 'Did I do the wrong thing?'

'I don't know,' said Alice. 'That dog, no matter how much trouble he was, he meant something to the kids. He represented mistakes and goof-ups. He made this perfect little palace an easier place to live in. Beethoven made this house real. He put dents in it.'

None of this was making George feel any better.

'Beethoven smelled bad,' Alice continued, 'and he slobbered, but he loved us. Even you. I hope you did this for the sake of the children, because I'd hate to think you sold Beethoven down the river for a chance to sell more air fresheners.'

George shook his head slowly. 'It wasn't about air fresheners. You saw what Beethoven did to the vet.'

'Yes, but we don't know why. Emily is really sticking to her story about the vet hitting Beethoven. She would never accuse an adult of lying if it wasn't true.'

George nodded. 'Yes, I know.'

'Then before we listen to some vet we don't know, maybe we ought to try listening to our child.'

'Maybe.'

'Something just doesn't make sense here. Can we just go and talk to the vet?'

George considered this for a moment. 'What am I going to say? "Dr Varnick, are you *sure* you didn't hit my dog?" And what's he going to say? "Gee, Mr Newton, I *just* remembered, I *did* hit your dog!"'

'It would just make me feel better if we went down there,' insisted Alice.

Just then, Ryce, Ted and Emily stepped out on to the terrace. 'We're coming with you,' said Ryce, speaking for all of them.

'OK,' said Mr Newton reluctantly. 'Let's go.'

*

The animal hospital was deserted when the Newton family got there. Dr Varnick was surprised – and a little nervous – when he saw them on the steps of the clinic.

'What can I do for you folks?'

'I'm sorry to bother you,' said George, 'but –'

'We want our dog back,' said Ryce.

'Where's Beethoven?' demanded Emily.

'I'm very, very sorry. It's too late. The dog has been destroyed.'

'No!' screamed the children.

'I was told it wasn't going to happen until tomorrow,' stammered Mr Newton.

Ryce had heard enough. She pushed past Dr Varnick and stormed into the clinic. He seized her by the shoulders. 'Where do you think you're going, young lady?'

'Let go of my daughter!' shouted Mr Newton angrily. As he grabbed the vet's arm, he could see that there was no longer a bandage there. Emily had been right after all! 'How's your arm?' he asked.

'I told you he was lying!' yelled Emily.

The whole family charged into the office.

'You can't come in here,' protested Varnick. 'This is private property. I'm calling the police.'

'Good idea. I'd love to talk to them.'

The kids were running round the offices, looking for Beethoven. But all the cages were empty.

'Where are all the animals?' demanded Mr Newton.

'I don't have to answer any of your questions,'

108

shouted Dr Varnick angrily. 'You ordered your dog to be destroyed and it was done. Now get out?'

George Newton grabbed Dr Varnick by the lapels and slammed him against a cage. 'Where's my dog?'

'Hit me and I'll have you put in gaol for assault and battery!'

Mr Newton paused, but was too angry to care. He thumped the doctor as hard as he could. Varnick flew backwards and collapsed on to a cage. The children watched with awestruck pride.

'Let's get out of here,' said George.

'Wow, Dad,' said Ted, 'you were totally awesome!'

'Radical!' said Emily.

'Totally,' agreed Ryce.

'Honey,' breathed Alice, 'I've never found you more attractive!'

'What do we do now?' asked Emily.

'Call the police,' said George. They went out and headed towards the phone box on the corner.

But the police just weren't interested in a crooked vet. They had more important things to worry about. 'No, I don't have any evidence. But if you just come down here. No! I won't wait until morning to file a report.' Mr Newton slammed down the phone. 'Now what?' he asked his family.

It took Dr Varnick a few minutes to recover from the punch, but the instant his head cleared, he was on the phone too. He reached Vernon at the Dandy Pup Pet Supply warehouse and yelled at him angrily.

'We're out of business,' he shouted. 'I'm coming down there right now. I want you to destroy *all* the evidence. Do you understand?'

He hung up and went and jumped in his car, zooming off, completely unaware that he was being followed by the whole Newton family!

CHAPTER NINETEEN

Dr Varnick pulled up at the Dandy Pup Pet Supply building and ran inside. The Newton car rolled to a stop a hundred yards behind him.

'OK,' said George Newton, 'he went in there. I'm going to have a look around.' He looked at his watch. 'It's nine-thirty now. If I'm not back in fifteen minutes, don't come after me. Call the police. Understand?'

Alice and the kids exchanged frightened looks. 'Are you sure?'

'I've got to,' said George. He got out of the car.

'Dad?' said Ryce.

'Yeah?'

'Good luck.'

'We're proud of you,' added Emily.

'Thanks.' George squared his shoulders and walked towards the warehouse like a sheriff in a Western movie. The big double doors of the building were locked tight. No way in there. There was only one thing to do. He started climbing the fire escape to the roof. George climbed up the iron ladder and looked in one of the big skylights.

He could see Dr Varnick filling a series of syringes and placing them carefully on a stainless-steel table.

'Before you destroy the dogs,' Varnick told

Vernon, 'bring me the St Bernard for the gun test, and a small one for some chemical tests.'

'Sure, Doc,' said Vernon. He hurried into the kennel room and grabbed Sparky out of his cage. The plucky little dog growled and bared his fangs.

Beethoven had stripped off his muzzle and was barking like crazy.

'Say goodbye to your pal, little guy!' said Vernon with a cruel smile as he headed for the operating room with Sparky.

Beethoven was not going to stand for this. He summoned up all his strength and threw himself against the rusty cage. The old metal couldn't stand up to the impact of one hundred and eighty-five pounds of angry dog.

Beethoven burst out of the cell and charged down the hall in hot pursuit of Sparky. Vernon was so surprised to see Beethoven that he dropped the little dog and turned on his attacker, beating him with the pole, and then snaring him with the cruel wire loop.

'Hold him!' ordered Dr Varnick. He quickly loaded the gun with the exploding ammunition and aimed it at Beethoven's head. 'This will teach you!'

At that very moment, George Newton crashed through the glass skylight roof and landed on Harvey, flattening him.

Dr Varnick was very calm about this intrusion. 'Nice of you to drop in, Mr Newton,' he said, levelling the gun at George. 'Now we'll *really* know if this ammo works.'

He cocked the gun.

Beethoven could do nothing. He was immobilized by the pole. George looked at the muzzle of the weapon and cringed.

'You have been very foolish, Mr Newton. You should have left when the going was good. A dog is not worth dying for.'

In the split second before Varnick pulled the trigger, Sparky came leaping out of nowhere, his teeth bared. His strong jaws clamped down hard on Varnick's crotch!

The vet screamed and fired at the same time. The bullet exploded on the concrete floor. Pandemonium erupted!

It was exactly 9.45 p.m. Mrs Newton got out of the car to look for a phone box. The fifteen minutes were up.

'You kids stay here,' she said nervously. She hurried down the alley towards the street.

The moment she turned the corner, the kids in the car heard a shot. Then another!

'Oh no!' shrieked Ryce. 'What are we going to do?'

Ted climbed into the front seat of the car. He knew exactly what to do. He straightened his glasses, turned the key in the ignition, and the engine burst into life. His feet could barely reach the pedals and he could hardly see over the wheel, but he was a young man with a mission. He revved the engine and shouted to his sisters.

'Buckle up! We're going in!'

He floored the accelerator and the big car jumped forward, heading straight for the doors of the warehouse.

CHAPTER TWENTY

The car hit the wooden garage doors of the Dandy Pup Pet Supply building like a cannon-ball. The front bumper slammed into the table holding the syringes and sent it flying. The dozen nasty needles sailed through the air and smacked into Dr Varnick's chest, injecting him with a variety of sedatives and tranquillizers. He looked like a human pin-cushion. He screamed loudly and then slid to the floor, out cold.

The operating room was a disaster-area of rubble and dust. Harvey and Vernon were nowhere to be seen.

George Newton hugged the children. 'Ted! Ryce! Emily! Are you OK?'

'Great!' exclaimed Ted.

'Where's Mom?'

Alice was climbing over the car that still blocked the main entrance. 'I called the police! They're on their way!'

'Thank goodness!' sighed George.

'Hey,' shouted Ryce. 'We've got to let these dogs out of their cages.'

'Yeah! Free the prisoners!'

'Well, maybe it would be better if we waited for the police to get here first,' said Mr Newton soberly.

'Awww, Dad,' said the Newton children.

'You're right! Let 'em out!' George cried.

The kids immediately ran to the cages and started throwing open the doors. In an instant, the room was knee-deep in barking canines.

Just then, Ted saw Vernon and Harvey trying to sneak out of a side entrance. He pointed. 'Get 'em, boys!'

The dogs needed no encouragement. Led by Sparky and Beethoven, they took off after their tormentors.

Vernon and Harvey saw the wave of dogs coming towards them and they fled, running down the alley as if their lives depended on it. They turned left on the main street and ran straight through the open-air market that stood next to the warehouse. They pushed their way through the crowd of people working in the market, tipping over crates as they went, hoping to put up enough obstacles to slow the dogs down.

Beethoven and Sparky led the charge through the piles of vegetables. Some dogs slipped and slid on the apples and cabbages, but the obstacles hardly slowed them down. The dogs were baying and barking, determined to get hold of the men who had treated them so cruelly.

Vernon looked over his shoulder and saw the four-footed pursuers gaining on them.

'We have to *do* something!'

'Look!'

They were out of the market now, running past a

scrapyard surrounded by a tall metal fence. Vernon threw himself against the gate and quickly clambered up, hauling himself to the top and dropping down on the other side. Harvey followed him, pulling himself up. Beethoven's jaws snapped just one inch short of his leg.

The two guys stood behind the fence while the dogs on the other side barked and howled and threw themselves at the chain-link fencing. But there was no way they could get at their prey.

'Shut up, you feeble-brained mongrels!' Vernon taunted. 'Thought you had me, huh? Well, never! No way.'

Harvey tapped him on the shoulder. 'Uh, Vernon.'

But Vernon had not finished tormenting the dogs. 'I'm not gonna forget about this. I'm going to get each and every one of you, understand?'

Harvey was tugging at his sleeve insistently. 'Vernon.'

Vernon turned impatiently. 'What? What is it?'

'Look,' said Harvey, pointing to something in the scrapyard.

Coming out from the heaps of rusting metal and debris were six big, mean, ugly Dobermann pinschers. Their fangs were bared and they growled, low and threatening. Their job was to protect the yard and they took their job very seriously.

'Uh-oh,' said Vernon.

CHAPTER TWENTY-ONE

It didn't take long for justice to catch up with Dr Varnick, Vernon and Harvey. Not long after the events at the Dandy Pup Pet Supply warehouse, the whole Newton family — Beethoven included, of course — gathered on the sitting-room sofa to watch the evening news.

'And the final chapter of a horror story for animal lovers concluded at the county courthouse today,' read the newscaster.

'Here it is!' shouted Ted.

The scene shifted to show a reporter on the courthouse steps.

'Animal lovers everywhere cheered today when Dr Herman Varnick and two associates were indicted on one hundred and twenty-three counts of animal abuse.'

The Newton family clapped and cheered, and they started booing as a handcuffed Dr Varnick was led down the courthouse steps, surrounded by a mob of reporters. In the background they could see two heavily bandaged figures — Harvey and Vernon — being hustled into a police car.

'I'm innocent!' Varnick yelled. 'These were legitimate scientific investigations!'

'No they weren't!' shouted Ryce.

The camera swung back to the reporter. 'And leading the cheers were the ring's captors, the Newton family of Vista Valley.'

The camera focused on the whole Newton family on the courthouse steps. George was wearing a suit, with the children dressed in their Sunday best. Beethoven was there too, his coat perfectly combed.

'Yayyyy!' shouted Ted.

Ryce blushed when she saw herself on the screen. 'Oh no! You can see my braces!'

The reporter interviewed Mrs Newton first. 'We're just happy that justice was served,' she said bashfully. 'And I'm very proud of my husband.'

'Well,' said the reporter, turning to Mr Newton, 'as a dog-owner myself, we all owe you a great debt.'

George did his best to look modest. 'Well,' he said, 'I only did what I would have done for any member of my family.'

Beethoven appreciated that. He barked happily.

The reporter wrapped up her story and Mr Newton stood up and snapped off the TV set.

'OK, kids,' said Alice. 'It's time for bed.'

Ted, Ryce and Emily lined up to kiss their father goodnight.

'Night, Dad,' said Ted, 'you're the best!'

'Goodnight, buddy. You too.'

Ryce threw her arms around her father's neck and hugged him close. 'Goodnight, Daddy. I love you.'

George beamed. 'Goodnight, sweetheart. I love you too.'

Emily wasn't quite ready to go to bed. 'Can I stay up?' she asked hopefully.

George gave her a kiss and sent her on her way. 'Goodnight, baby.'

Just then, the phone rang. George answered it and listened for a moment. 'Ryce, it's for you. Don't talk too long. It's bedtime.'

'I won't. Who is it?'

'A friend who says he saw you on TV. Said his name was Mark something.'

Ryce's eyes grew wide. 'Mark?'

'That's right. Goodnight, sweetheart.'

The whole house was settled in bed. Alice snuggled against her husband.

'Goodnight, honey,' she said.

George kissed her. 'Sleep tight.'

There was a bark from the dark.

'Goodnight, Beethoven,' said George. Beethoven was sleeping at the end of the bed.

Then there was another bark!

'Goodnight, Sparky.'

Sparky was sleeping on the floor next to the bed.

Another bark. A basset hound was sleeping next to Sparky.

'Goodnight, Maggie.'

George sat up. 'Might as well say goodnight to all of you. Goodnight, Cindy. Goodnight, Hawkeye. Goodnight, Bobo. Goodnight, Ruthie.'

The whole room was full of dogs!

RUN SWIFT, RUN FREE
Tom McCaughren

Summer has come to the land of Sinna, and the new foxcubs are growing up. They as yet know nothing of the terrible dangers faced by their parents in recent times, and have much to learn before they can safely fend for themselves.

The final part of this award-winning trilogy, which began with *Run With the Wind* and *Run to Earth*, follows the adventures of the young foxes as a new generation learns to survive in a hostile world, and to run swift, run free.

WHO EVER HEARD OF A VEGETARIAN FOX?
Rosalind Kerven

Sarah and her sister Caroline both care passionately about animals but their new home is surrounded by traps and snares set by the gamekeeper and they set about a campaign of sabotage. Then they make friends with Ian, the gamekeeper's son. His arguments for the gamekeeper are just as convincing as Caroline's are against, and Sarah finds herself caught between the two or them.

ADAM'S ARK
Paul Stewart

'Who are you?' Adam thought out loud ...
'The name's Oscar,' the cat thought back.

Oscar's arrival in the house has a dramatic effect on Adam. For in discovering that he can think-talk with the cat, he is at last able to break free of the autistic-like state he has been living in. But the more he learns about the sad plight of animals everywhere, the more he wonders why he alone of humans has this extraordinary ability to communicate with them.

FLOWER OF JET

Bell Mooney

It's the time of the miner's strike. Tom Farrell's father is branded with the word Tom most dreads; Melanie Wall's father is the strike leader. How can Tom and Melanie's friendship survive the violence and bitterness of both sides? Things are to grow far worse than they ever imagined, for Melanie and Tom discover a treacherous plot that could destroy both their families. And they have to act fast if they're going to stop it.

MIGHTIER THAN THE SWORD

Clare Bevan

Adam had always felt he was somehow special, different from the rest of the family, but could he really be a modern-day King Arthur, the legendary figure they're learning about at school? Inspired by the stories they are hearing in class, Adam and his friends become absorbed in a complex game of knights and good deeds. All they need is a worthy cause for which to fight. So when they discover that the local pond is under threat, Adam's knights are ready to join battle with the developers.

Reality and legend begin to blur in this lively, original story about an imaginative boy who doesn't let a mere wheelchair get in his way of adventure.

AGAINST THE STORM

Gaye Hicyilmaz

'As Mehmet is drawn into his parents' ill-considered scheme to go and live in Ankara, the directness and the acute observation of Gaye Hicyilmaz carry the reader with him ... Terrible things happen: illness, humiliation, death. But Mehmet is a survivor, and as the book closes, "a sort of justice" has been done, and a satisfying victory achieved. It is a sort of justice too ... that in all the dire traffic of unpublishable manuscripts something as fresh and powerful as this should emerge' — *The Times*

THE BEST-KEPT SECRET
Emily Rodda

The arrival of the fairground carousel, surrounded by its neat red and white painted fence, with a tent guarding its entrance, was a complete mystery to the residents of Marley Street. Where had it come from? How it had appeared so quickly? And why was the music so haunting, beckoning all to come and look? Jo is determined to have a ride, even though she senses the ride may take her into danger, into an unknown world . . . the world of the future.

THE TOBY MAN
Dick King-Smith

Young Tod Golightly knows what a highwayman *should* say and do, but finds it's more difficult than it sounds. Being so young and inexperienced, people don't take him seriously. Then he gathers about himself a team of unlikely accomplices — a wise old donkey, a large dog, a magpie and a cunning ferret. Together they pull off a daring robbery, which turns Tod into the terror of the Great West Road. But the Bow Street Runners are after this dangerous criminal and determined to make him pay — with his life. How will his animal friends be able to help him now?

BIG IGGY
Kaye Umansky

When Large Lizzy decides it's time she had a bit of peace and quiet, Big Iggy — the smallest dragon — and his brothers all take off into the big wide world. But Big Iggy's first flight ends with a crash landing into a tree — and a huge adventure.

A RIVER RAN OUT OF EDEN
James Vance Marshall

Young Eric seeks shelter from a terrible storm which sweeps across the island, and discovers a rare and beautiful gold-furred seal. A warm friendship grows between the boy and the animal but their friendship is threatened by two men who want to kill the golden seal for her valuable fur. One of the men is Eric's father, whom he loves and trusts; the other is a stranger who plots against Eric's father and tries to come between his parents.

WILD!
Rosalind Kerven

The Rushing family have developed an astonishing rapport with the wild animals who share their remote mountain home. But the beautiful wilderness is about to be destroyed and turned into an enormous theme park. Dave and Emma, their friends from London, are determined to save Old Mountain. And who better to help them than the charismatic pop-star, Wild Man? Soon the campaign reaches national television — and suddenly a lot of accepted ideas about animals are turned upside-down.